GalaxyQuest

Galaxy Quest
Junior Novelization

by **Ellen Weiss**

adapted from a screenplay by
Robert Gordon

based on a story by
David Howard and **Robert Gordon**

DREAMWORKS™

PUFFIN BOOKS
Published by the Penguin Group
Penguin Putnam Books for Young Readers, 345 Hudson Street,
New York, NY 10014, U.S.A.
Penguin Books Ltd, 27 Wrights Lane, London W8 5TZ, England
Penguin Books Australia Ltd, Ringwood, Victoria, Australia
Penguin Books Canada Ltd, 10 Alcorn Avenue, Toronto, Ontario, Canada M4V 3B2
Penguin Books (N.Z.) Ltd, 182-190 Wairau Road, Auckland 10, New Zealand

Penguin Books Ltd, Registered Offices: Harmondsworth, Middlesex, England

Published by Puffin Books,
a member of Penguin Putnam Books for Young Readers, 1999

1 3 5 7 9 10 8 6 4 2

ISBN 0-14-130743-9

Printed in the United States of America

Introduction

The magnificent starship rumbled through the vastness of space, its enormous hull starkly lit by an alien sun. The letters emblazoned on the side read NSEA PROTECTOR.

As the ship hurtled through the emptiness, it shuddered slightly. Inside the *Protector*'s instrument-filled cabin, the crew exchanged relieved smiles.

"We're exiting the time knot now, sir!" reported youthful Lieutenant Laredo to the Commander. Even though he was only nine years old, he served as both the *Protector*'s navigator and its gunner.

"We're alive," said Tech Sergeant Chen joyfully.

"We made it. Commander, we made it!" whooped young Laredo.

Dr. Lazarus, the ship's only alien crew member, stepped forward, bowing his great purple, reptilian-looking head. "By Grabthar's hammer," he said gravely, "we live to tell the tale."

"Systems register functional," intoned the computer.

"All systems are working, Commander," confirmed beautiful shipmate Tawny Madison fetchingly. "Commander?"

They all looked toward the Commander, who turned slowly, to reveal himself in the most impressive possible way. He was a good-looking fellow and he knew it. He looked around the command deck, worried, practically sniffing the air.

"I don't like it," said the Commander ominously. "It was too easy. Look for ambient energy fields," he ordered.

"All normal, sir," reported Laredo, pushing a plastic button. "The entire spectrum."

"Check again, Laredo," said the Commander.

"Yes, sir, I—wait. Oh no." Laredo's radar was lighting up with dots. First a few, then hundreds. "They're everywhere. There are time knots opening everywhere," he said, panic-stricken. "*Impact now*, Commander!"

An explosion rocked the ship.

"A trap," said Tawny Madison bitterly.

"We're surrounded, Commander," said Laredo. "The entire 5K Ranking is out there."

"Our plasma armor?" inquired the Commander.

"Gone, sir." Another blast rocked the room.

"Structural damage at sixty-eight percent," said the computer's pleasant voice.

"We're sustaining major structural damage!"echoed Tawny.

"It's a core meltdown, sir. It can't be stopped!" cried Tech Sergeant Chen.

The Commander turned to his advisor, the solemn Dr. Lazarus.

"Commander, surrender may be our only option," said Lazarus in a British accent that was particularly magnificent for an alien lizard-creature.

"No!" said the Commander bravely. "Never give up. Never surrender!"

Tawny consulted the computer. "The reactor has eaten through four levels . . . Six levels . . . The ship is disintegrating!" she said.

"Your orders, sir?" beseeched young Laredo. "Sir, your orders?"

The Commander stepped forward so that the camera would get a nice close-up shot of the steely determination on his face. "Activate the Omega 13," he said.

The crewmates exchanged expectant and terrified glances as five layers of mechanical locks were opened, revealing an extremely serious-looking lever. The Commander stepped forward. He pulled the lever, and at once a large machine rose from the floor in the middle of the room. It began to glow, brighter and brighter. The brightness filled the room until, suddenly, everything went white.

Black numbers appeared, along with a studio copyright notice.

In the audience at the science fiction convention, hundreds of enthralled fans, mostly spotty-faced teenage boys, continued to stare at the larger-than-life screen. For a moment all was silent. Then there was a burst of thunderous applause and cheering.

Guy, the master of ceremonies, took the stage. "Well, there you are!" he said enthusiastically. "You are the first people to see the lost *Galaxy Quest* Episode Fifty-two two-parter since it was originally aired in '82! As most of you know, no concluding episode was filmed when the series was canceled, so the episode was never included in the syndication run. Let's hear it for Travis Latke, who actually rescued the footage from the studio garbage!

"Now," the master of ceremonies continued, "for the moment you've all been waiting for . . . the intrepid crew of the NSEA *Protector*!"

But the intrepid crew was not quite ready to come

out. In the wings, a stagehand was frantically signaling for Guy to stretch out his introduction.

And so, Guy began to vamp. "But first," he said, trying desperately to think of something to talk about, "what is a 'hero'? Let's take a look at a few more clips . . ."

Backstage, the *Galaxy Quest* actors were waiting. They were all dressed in their funny-looking, uncomfortable futuristic outfits, and they were not happy.

"Where the hell is he?" grumbled Tommy Webber, the youngest of the group, who had played the role of Laredo. "An hour and a half late. An hour and a half!"

Gwen Demarco, also known as Tawny Madison, was pacing the room in a tight, sexy body suit. "This is great," she said, looking through the curtain. "They're going to start eating each other out there."

Alexander Dane, the classically trained British actor who played Dr. Lazarus was sitting in front of a lighted mirror, regarding his purple alien makeup and scaly rubber features with a mournful expression.

"Oh, and did you hear he booked another fan appearance without us?" groused Tommy.

"You're kidding," said Gwen. "When for?"

"Tomorrow morning, before the store opening," Tommy replied.

"The guy is terminally selfish!" Gwen agreed.

Fred Kwan, alias Tech Sergeant Chen, was staring intently at a 3D picture that he had picked up on his way into the convention hall, trying to bring the hidden image into focus. "He ate my sandwich," he said, looking up.

"What?" said Gwen and Tommy.

"A month ago, he ate my sandwich."

"And he ate Fred's *sandwich*!" said Tommy in outrage.

Gwen noticed that Alexander was still staring into the mirror. "Oh Alex, get away from that thing," she said.

But he could not take his eyes from his depressing reflection. "Dear God," he said theatrically. "How did I come to this?"

"Not again." Tommy sighed.

"I played Richard the Third . . ."

"Five curtain calls . . ." Fred chimed in under his breath.

"Five curtain calls!" Alexander went on, not noticing. "I was an *actor* once, damn it. Now look at me . . . *look at me*."

"Settle down, Alex," said Tommy.

"No. I can't go out there!" shouted Alexander. "I won't say that ridiculous catch phrase one more time. I won't. I can't!"

"At least you had a *part*," said Gwen sourly. "You had a character people loved! My *TV Guide* interview was six paragraphs about this body suit. About my legs. Nobody ever bothered to ask what I *do* on the ship."

"You were the, uh . . . Wait, I'll think of it," said Fred vaguely.

"I repeated the computer! 'It's getting hotter, Commander!' 'The ship is disintegrating, Commander!' Nothing I did *ever* affected the plot, not *once*! Nothing I did was ever taken seriously!"

"Excuse me," interrupted Tommy. "I'm an African-American playing a nine-year-old Malaysian named Laredo. Hello!"

Suddenly, the door opened and Jason Nesmith strolled in: the Commander, all exuberance and charm. He immediately began working the room.

"My friends," he announced cheerfully, "your Commander has arrived! Am I too late for Alexanders's panic attack?" He looked at Alexander. "Apparently so." He chuckled. He cast his eyes quickly over the group, stopping on Gwen. "You look spectacular," he said, admiringly.

At last he noticed that they were all glaring at him. "Oh, what did I do now?" he asked.

Out on the convention stage, Guy was continuing to stall. "Sure, the rocks looked hollow and the sets moved when anyone bumped into them," he said. "But we didn't care . . ."

Behind him, clips from the show were being projected on a large screen. On an alien planet, the Commander carried the limp body of his advisor, Lazarus, as ray guns erupted around him.

"For those four seasons," Guy continued, "from '79 to '82, we the viewers developed the same affection for the crew of the NSEA *Protector* that the crew had for each other. These weren't just adventurers exploring space, these were friends . . ."

Meanwhile, the "friends" were fighting backstage. They surrounded Jason in a fury. "You said we do appearances together, or not at all!" yelled Tommy.

"I didn't say that. I said 'Wouldn't it be great if we could always work together.' *That's* what I said."

"You are so full of it," said Tommy.

Jason looked deeply offended that they could think such a thing of him. "A few fans built a little set in their garage. I come in for an hour at most. It's a nothing," he protested.

"How much of a nothing?" Gwen demanded. "Not enough to split five ways kind of a nothing?"

Jason shrugged. "What do you want me to say, Gwen? They wanted the Commander."

Suddenly they noticed a bright light was streaming in, and turned to see Alexander skulking out the exit. They all ran to catch him, tackling him.

Onstage, Guy was still tap-dancing. Then, at last, he got a thumbs-up cue from a stagehand and began to introduce the cast, to the delight of the applauding fans.

"Okay, here we go . . . Let's hear a warm welcome for crack Gunner/Navigator Laredo, Tommy Webber!"

Tommy came bounding out with a big smile. A film clip of young Laredo in action was playing on the screen behind him. "If it's got quantum rockets," Tommy's character was saying, "I can fly it."

As the crowd cheered, Guy made his next introduction: "Ship's Tech Sergeant Chen . . . Fred Kwan!"

Fred strolled out with a casual wave. Behind him, on the big screen, Chen was saying, "Give me a stick of gum and a hairpin and we're on our way!"

Meanwhile, backstage, Gwen and Jason were still wrestling on the ground with Alexander.

"Alex, you can't just leave!" Gwen entreated him.

"Oh, can't I? Watch me!"

"Come on, old friend," Jason cajoled.

That was too much for Alexander. "'Old friend'!" he spat out. "You stole all my best lines. You cut me out of Episode Three entirely!"

Guy was blithely continuing with the introductions onstage. "The beautiful shipmate Tawny Madison . . . Gwen Demarco!"

Gwen sprinted out onto the stage, noticeably ruffled. In the film clip behind her, Tawny Madison was looking around the cabin fearfully.

"One hundred degrees and rising . . ." said the computer.

"It's . . . it's getting hotter, Commander!" parroted Gwen as Tawny.

There were many appreciative whistles from audience. Gwen forced a smile.

"And now," said Guy, "the Commander's advisor and closest friend. His peaceful nature ever at odds with the savage warrior inside him . . ."

Behind Guy played a split-screen clip of Alexander as Dr. Lazarus. On one side he was the mild-mannered British reptile-creature, on the other a savage beast of vengeance, tearing into a foe.

At that moment, Alexander was more like the second Dr. Lazarus. He was still in a wrestling match with Jason.

"You *will* go out there," Jason said through gritted teeth.

"I won't, and nothing you say can change—"

But Jason knew the one thing that would change Alexander's mind. It was part of his training. "The show must go on," he cried.

"Damn you! Damn you!" spat Alexander, helpless in the face of the magic show-business incantation.

"Dr. Lazarus of Tev'meck . . . Alexander Dane!" they heard Guy say.

Alex bounded up onto the stage, bowing deeply with grace and humility—always the stage-trained British actor.

On the screen behind him, Dr. Lazarus was uttering the same old line: "By Grabthar's hammer, you shall be avenged!" Alex cringed, desperately unhappy.

"And finally, my fellow Questarians," Guy announced jubilantly, "the brave Commander of the NSEA *Protector*,

Peter Quincy Taggart—*Jason Nesmith!*"

As Jason appeared, a spotlight followed him on. The other actors just stared.

"Unbelievable," whispered Tommy. "He rented a *spot*?"

Jason raised his fist in the air, encouraging the fans to cry out the Commander's classic words along with him, and along with his triumphal figure on the screen: *"Never give up, never surrender . . . Damn the resonance cannons, full speed ahead!"*

The fans, of course, went crazy, as the actors exchanged glances.

Guy cried out his last announcement over the continued cheers of the frenzied crowd. "The Commander and his crew will be signing autographs on Imperial Decks B and C near the Coke machines!"

At that moment, in the deserted convention center hallway, five serious-looking young people, four men and a woman, were walking in lock-step toward the convention floor. They were clean-cut, impeccably outfitted in perfect *Galaxy Quest* uniforms. But there was something odd about them. Something hard to define.

The peculiar fans entered the bustling convention floor, making their way through hordes of others decked out as their favorite *Galaxy Quest* characters. They moved past the rows of booths selling *Galaxy Quest* and other sci-fi memorabilia. At one booth, a group of particularly earnest teenage fans, also costumed as the five *Galaxy Quest* leads, were standing at a vendor's booth. Their fourteen-year-old leader, Brandon Wheeger, was contemptuously inspecting a seller's model of the *Protector*.

"The tail fin is concave, not convex," he informed the hapless seller. "The proton reactor is where the influx thermistors should be and—my God—is this Testor's blue-green number six on the hull?" He dropped the model roughly. "I . . . I . . . This is a complete abomination."

Glancing curiously at this similarly uniformed group, the peculiar fans moved along. They came to a halt as soon as they spotted Jason, who was up on a raised platform at the front of the hall, signing autographs for a long line of fans.

The peculiar fans stared at Jason as if they were in the presence of God. They exchanged astonished smiles and then started toward him.

Up front, Gwen, Tommy, Alexander, and Fred were signing autographs at a row of tables near Jason. It had not escaped them that their seats were significantly lower than his perch.

"Is it me," Tommy asked nobody in particular, "or does his table get higher at every convention?"

One of the many fans dressed as Dr. Lazarus stepped up to Alexander and saluted him with crossed fists. "By Grabthar's hammer," vowed the fan, "by the suns of Warvan, I shall avenge you!"

Alexander simply ignored this performance. He grabbed the photo from the fan's hand, signed it, and thrust it back.

The next fan stepped up. "By Grabthar's hammer, by the—" he began. Alex signed the photo and shoved it back toward him before he could finish.

Along came Guy, the convention's emcee. "Hi, everybody," he said.

"Hey," Tommy responded. "Thanks for the nice intro, uh . . ."

"Guy," Guy reminded him. "You probably don't remember me, do you? I was on the show in '82. Episode Thirty-one? Got killed by the lava monster before the first commercial? Crewman Number Six?"

"Oh, right! Guy!" said all the actors, madly pretending to remember him.

"Listen," said Guy, "I was wondering, would you guys mind if I sit in today? See if anybody's interested in an autograph? You never know."

"Sure, Guy," said Gwen drily. "If you can stand the excitement."

Meanwhile, two more fans dressed as Dr. Lazarus were approaching Alexander, brightly chattering at him in the Mak'tar language.

"Don't make me get a restraining order," he told them disgustedly.

Across the room, the peculiar fans were making their way through the crowd. If anyone had been looking closely, they might have seen something very strange. The left hand of the tallest one was flickering between a normal hand and a hand with seven long blue tentacles for fingers.

But before anyone else could notice, the leader spotted the problem and motioned to the afflicted fellow. He rapped sharply against a blinking metal box on his belt and the hand became normal again.

Up at the cast table, Guy sat with the others, looking forlorn. No fans were in line for his autograph.

A teenage boy stepped up to Gwen and handed her a picture to sign. "I'm a big fan, Ms. Demarco," he gushed.

Gwen looked at the photo. "You really expect me to sign a naked picture?" she spluttered. "This isn't even my body!"

"Yeah," replied the fan, unfazed, "normally with fakes it's like, recycle bin. But this one's really good."

Gwen sighed and signed the picture.

At last, it was Guy's big moment: a fan was approaching! Guy looked up eagerly. The fan looked at him quizzically, trying to place him.

"Episode Thirty-one," said Guy. He got no reaction. "Killed by the lava monster?" he said helpfully.

The fan simply turned away without a word and approached Tommy. "Laredo, could I get an autograph?" he asked.

Gwen gave Guy a comforting look, then looked across at Jason, who was up on his perch, talking dramatically to a group of fans.

"On one hand," he was declaiming, "if I had moved an inch, the beast would have killed me. On the other hand, my crew was in danger . . ."

"How did you know what to do?" asked a pretty fan, spellbound.

"Without a crew, I'm not a commander," said Jason with a wink.

"And we all know what happened to that beast on Enok 7," he added.

The fans all made happy, nerdy "we sure do" noises.

Gwen watched this performance, shaking her head appreciatively. "You gotta admit, they do love him," she said, a smile creeping across her face.

"Almost as much as he loves himself," said Tommy, watching as Jason fielded another question from a fan.

Bored with the constant queries of his fans, Jason glanced over to see Gwen still smiling at him. She quickly looked away, self-conscious. But Jason didn't take his eyes off her.

Brandon now stepped forward, his brow knitted with serious matters. "Commander," he said, "please settle a dispute that my crew and I are having."

Jason, however, was elsewhere. "Excuse me, guys," he said, standing up.

"But—but I hadn't even gotten to the relevant conundrum," protested Brandon.

Jason didn't hear him, though. He was already headed toward Gwen's table, where she was answering a question from a shy girl.

"Miss Demarco?" the girl was saying. "In Episode Fifteen, 'Mist of Delos 5'? I got the feeling you and the

Commander kind of had a *thing* in the swamp when you were stranded together. Did you?"

"The Commander and I *never* had a thing," snapped Gwen.

"That's her story," Jason cut in.

Gwen looked up sharply to find a smiling Jason standing beside her. The girl took this as her cue to make herself scarce, giggling.

"What?" Gwen demanded of Jason.

"You smiled at me."

Rolling her eyes, Gwen rose and walked off.

Jason followed, undaunted, and immediately ran smack into the five aliens disguised as fans. Their leader bowed respectfully, then followed along, oblivious to the fact that Jason was pursuing Gwen.

"Commander," said the alien, "I must speak to you. My name is Mathesar. We are Thermians from the Klatu Nebula, and we require your help."

Jason waved him away impatiently, assuming he was just another obsessed fan with an overactive imagination. "Right, if this is about the thing tomorrow you can hammer out the details with my agent, but make sure I have a limo from my house. They jammed me into a Toyota the last time I did one of these."

"I . . . Certainly, but—" said Mathesar, confused.

"Catch me later, okay?" and off he sped to catch up to Gwen.

When he was beside her, he spun her around to face

him. "Crewman Madison," he said dramatically, "I . . . I'm sorry. Whatever I do next I have no control over. It's the mist on this strange planet, it's filling my head with such *thoughts* . . ."

He leaned toward her for a tortured screen-style kiss. Meanwhile, some fans had gathered, delighted by the impromptu show.

But Gwen quickly stepped aside. "It was cute when I didn't know you," she said.

Jason tried to pretend that it hadn't hurt as she turned on her heel and walked away. But it did hurt, and he needed to find a place to be alone, without the horde of yelling, grabbing fans.

He went to the men's room.

But even the men's room was no refuge. It was full of fans dressed in Mank'nar Beast costumes, trying to figure out how to use the bathroom. Jason fled into an empty stall. But even there, he got no peace. Two young men had entered the bathroom, laughing hysterically.

"You're right!" screeched one. "What a freak show. This is hilarious! Those poor actors. They've done, like, *what* for twenty years?"

"Yeah, the Laredo guy is still like 'Gee whiz, proton thrusters, I can fly it,'" added the other, in a little boy voice. "And the tech guy," he went on, "total burnout."

"Did you hear Nesmith up there? I think he actually gets off on these nerds thinking he's Space Commander.

It's pathetic. And his friends . . ."

"Did you hear them ragging on him?"

The two young cynics erupted in fresh laughter. "He has no idea that he's a laughingstock," said the first, giggling. "Even to his buddies."

They left the bathroom, their voices ringing in Jason's ears.

Jason returned to the table in a foul mood. He scribbled his name irritably, trying to avoid contact with the fans. But Brandon and his group were heading toward him.

"Commander," said Brandon, "as I was saying . . . In 'The Quasar Dilemma,' you used the auxiliary of deck B for gamma override. But online blueprints indicate that the auxiliary of deck B is independent of the guidance matrix. So we were wondering where the error lies?"

Jason lost it. He just couldn't keep up the charade any longer. "It's a television show. Okay? That's all! It's just a bunch of fake sets and wooden props! Do you understand?" he shouted.

"Yes, but we were wondering—" Brandon persisted.

"There *is* no quantum flux and there is no auxiliary! There's no ship! Do you get it?" Jason roared.

All at once, Jason noticed that the hall had become deathly quiet. All eyes were turned on him.

He rose abruptly and made his way through the hall to the exit, as Brandon and the other fans did their best not to take the tirade they'd just heard personally.

Later that night, Gwen and Alex were talking on the phone.

"I don't know, Alex," said Gwen, keeping the phone tucked beneath her chin as she bustled about her kitchen, cooking dinner. "He's never gone quite this far before."

Alexander, sitting at his kitchen table, was using spirit gum in an effort to remove his alien head appliance. "I've said it for years, Gwen," he said into the phone. "He's mentally unstable."

Standing up, he went to the refrigerator. It was not good news. Nothing but a hunk of very rank cheese. He made a face.

"I don't know," Gwen was saying. "It just wasn't like Jason."

"Yes, poor Jason. Probably out, a girl in each arm, spinning yarns to a roomful of attractive hangers-on. While here I sit eating Christmas cheese in spring."

Nothing could have been further from the truth, however. At that moment, Jason was sitting on the edge of his bed, staring at the TV, sipping a drink and flipping channels. He stopped at the conclusion of an episode of *Galaxy Quest*. As Commander Taggart made a heroic speech, Jason mouthed the words along with his alter ego.

"As long as there is injustice," vowed Jason and Commander Taggart together, "whenever a Targathian baby cries out, wherever a distress signal sounds among the stars . . . we'll be there. This fine ship, and this fine crew . . . Never give up! Never surrender!"

In seconds, Jason was passed out on his bed, face down in a pillow, his body twisted in misery.

Jason was still out cold, dead to the world, when his doorbell rang the next morning. He groaned and pulled a pillow over his head as it rang and rang. Finally there was nothing to do but get out of bed, drag on a robe, and answer the door.

There, standing before him, were the aliens, in regulation *Galaxy Quest* attire. Jason squinted at them out of bloodshot eyes. He had a bad headache. With earnest and respectful faces, the five saluted him in classic *Galaxy Quest* style.

Jason shut the door in their earnest and respectful faces.

The bell rang again.

Jason ripped the door open. *"What. Do. You. Want?!"* he shouted.

The leader, Mathesar, stepped forward and spoke quickly. "Sir," he said, "I understand this is a terrible breach of protocol, but please, I beg you to hear our plea. We are Thermians from the Klatu Nebula. Our people are being systematically hunted and slaughtered by Roth'h'ar

Sarris of Fatu-Krey. Sarris wants the Omega 13. We are to meet in negotiation. However, our past efforts in this regard have been nothing short of disastrous. The flames, the death . . ."

He shuddered, then quickly gathered himself again. "Please, Captain, you are our last hope." Then he added, as Jason kept staring blankly, "We have secured a limousine."

"Oh, right!" said Jason, finally remembering them. "The thing with the thing. Come on in, I'll get some pants on."

The aliens stepped inside and waited politely as Jason got dressed.

"Commander, sir," said Mathesar, bending down toward Jason, who was rummaging under the sofa, "I speak for all of us when I say that standing here in your presence is the greatest honor we could ever have hoped to achieve in our lifetimes."

'Thanks, appreciate it . . . Anybody seen my other shoe?" asked Jason.

At last, Jason was dressed, and they were off. Half-awake, the actor sat in the back seat with Mathesar and the others.

"Sir," said one of the aliens, "I am Neru, senior requisition officer. Before we travel to the ship, please let me know if you have any requirements—weapons, documents, personnel . . ."

"I could use a Coke," said Jason.

The alien made a note.

Then another one spoke up. "Sir, I am Teb. I would like to explain the history between our people and the Sarris dominion in greater detail. In the five million years following the great nebula burst, our people were one . . ."

Jason interrupted, pointing at the fourth alien. "What about him?" he said. "Doesn't he talk?"

"His translator is broken," Teb explained.

The fourth alien attempted to say something, but it came out a weird mix of sounds, rather like a screaming baby inside a bagpipe.

Jason sighed. This bunch was certainly serious about their sci-fi. Well, might as well play it their way. "Okey-doke . . . so, listen," he said, "I had a late night with a Kreemorian fangor beast, so I'm going to shut my eyes for a bit. But go on, I'm listening to every word . . ."

In a second, he was asleep.

When Jason opened his eyes, he was being shaken softly by a pretty young woman in a *Galaxy Quest* uniform. In the background, he heard a low rumble.

"I am sorry to wake you, sir, but your presence is requested on the command deck. My name is Laliari. I will lead you there."

As Laliari escorted him down the high-tech hallway, Jason looked around, absently holding a can of Coke. He was trying to get his bearings.

"Sir, Sarris has moved the deadline," explained Laliari. "We are approaching his ship at the Ni-delta now. He wants an answer. I understand you have been briefed."

"Yeah, I got most of it in the car. He's the bad guy, right?"

"Yes, sir, he is a very bad man indeed. He has tortured our scientists, put us to work in the gallium-arsenide mines, captured our females for his own demented purposes . . ."

"Okay," Jason interrupted. "I've got the picture. You have pages or do you want me to just go for it?" These publicity appearances were really so tiresome.

Laliari was confused. "I'm not sure I . . ."

"Script pages. Never mind, let's see what old Sarris has to say for himself."

Mathesar and the other crew members were now heading toward them. "Commander," said Mathesar, "welcome to the *Protector II*. Would you like to don your uniform?"

"Mind if we skip that?" said Jason. "I have to get back pretty quick for this thing in Van Nuys."

"As you wish."

Their conversation was cut short as another crew member came running up. "Sir!" he panted. "It's Sarris. He's *here*!"

A door slid open before them, and suddenly Jason found himself on the command deck. It was straight out of the TV show—blinking lights, consoles, the cool technical displays. It was just a bit dark. But Jason was genuinely impressed as he looked about.

"Not bad," he told them. "Usually it's painted cardboard boxes in a garage."

"Sir, we apologize for operating in low power mode," said Teb, leading Jason to the Commander's chair. "But we are experiencing a reflective flux field this close to the galactic axis."

Jason took his seat. "No problem," he said. "This thing have a cup holder?"

The crew member who had reported Sarris's presence handed Jason a clipboard. "The situational analysis, Commander," he said.

"What's your name?" Jason asked him.

"Glath, sir," said the fellow, perplexed.

Jason signed his autograph and handed it back. "There you go," he said magnanimously.

The navigator turned to Jason. "We're approaching in five ticks, sir," he reported. "Command to slow?"

Jason looked toward the front window and saw the stars moving past in a familiar display.

"Sure, set the screen saver on two," he joked.

The navigator looked confused.

"Sorry. Sorry," Jason apologized. "Didn't mean to break the mood. Slow to Mark Two, Lieutenant."

A ship appeared before them, growing closer. It was

a menacing craft, sharp and jagged, with a gargoyle-shaped figurehead. Then the viewscreen came fuzzily to life, revealing an image of . . . Eeeew.

This guy was not pretty. He was ugly and green, with black sharp teeth. He had a metal hand.

There was a moment's silence as the crew members took in the sight, trying to well their courage.

"I see fear," Sarris hissed. "That is expected." His voice resonated throughout the cabin. "Ah, they bring a new Commander . . . Such a cowardly species. Not even your own kind. No matter. Here are my demands. Commander, I suggest that you think well before speaking a word, because these negotiations are—tender. If I do not like what I hear, there will be blood and pain as you cannot imagine . . ."

Jason took a sip of Coke and checked his watch.

"First," said Sarris, "I require the Omega 13. Second—"

Jason cut him off, wanting to move this gig along. "Okey-dokey," he said to the crew. "Let's fire blue particle cannons full. Fire red particle cannons full. Fire gannet magnets left and right. Fire pulse catapults from all chutes. And throw this thing at him too, killer." He handed the gunner the empty Coke can.

And then, before even waiting for the weapons to reach their targets, he turned and walked off the control deck, leaving the crew to exchange stunned glances as they tried to absorb the magnitude of what had just happened.

Out in the corridor, Jason looked both ways, trying to find the exit.

Mathesar and a few of the others caught up to him. "Commander? Where are you—going?" Mathesar asked.

"Home."

"You—you mean *Earth*?"

Jason had had just about enough of their little serious-fan game. "Yeah. 'Earth.' Time to get back to Earth, kids." Oblivious to the muffled sounds of the explosions outside, he kept walking.

"But, Commander," Mathesar protested, "the negotiation—you—you—you fired on him!"

"Right," Jason replied brusquely. "Long live . . . What's your planet?"

"Theramin."

"Long live Theramin!" said Jason. "Take a left here?"

"But what if Sarris survives?" Mathesar pleaded.

"Oh, I don't think you have to worry about that. I gave him both barrels."

"He has a very powerful ship," Mathesar fretted. "Perhaps you would like to wait to see the results of—"

"I would, but I am *really* running late," Jason interrupted. "If the guy gives you any more trouble, just give me a call."

Mathesar looked very unpersuaded, but nonetheless,

he produced a walkie-talkie device and handed it to Jason. "An interstellar vox," he said.

"Thanks," said Jason fliply.

Mathesar looked him in the eye, a tear starting down his cheek. He shook Jason's hand sincerely. "How can we thank you, Commander?" he said. "You—you have saved our people."

Jason smiled his most photogenic smile. "It was a lot of fun," he said. "You kids are great."

The other crew members gathered around him and shook his hand, thanking him as they ushered him out. But instead of an exit, he found that they had led him into a room with a very high circular ceiling.

Suddenly he realized that he was all alone. He was standing on a glowing red disk in the center of this strange room, which had no visible doors.

"Wait!" he cried. "Where's the car?"

Suddenly, a clear cylinder rose from the disk. It wrapped itself around him, encasing him in a transparent, bullet-shaped container. The ceiling divided and the walls pulled back around him, revealing a rotating starfield. It was awesome.

Jason had no time to react as his pod was rocketed forward into space.

And then, in the blink of an eye, he was standing on the red disk in the middle of his own backyard. Just like that.

He stood there in shock, shivering in waves from the

incomprehensibility of what he'd just experienced.

At that very moment, Brandon Wheeger and his forlorn group of friends were sitting in Brandon's garage. They were proudly wearing their best uniforms, and they had been so excited for the Commander to see the spaceship interior they'd made, using painted cardboard boxes and Christmas lights. Now they were very, very disappointed.

The next morning was the grand opening of the computer store. Gwen, Tommy, Fred, Alexander, and Guy were on hand for the festivities. A small crowd had gathered to inspect the store's mock-up of the *Protector*. Brandon and his gang were among them.

"Take it from us," said Gwen, reading from her script. "We've been all over the universe . . ."

"But we've never seen the space-age values," Fred continued, "that we've seen here at . . ."

"Tech Value Electronics Superstore!" Tommy finished.

Alexander paused, deeply ashamed, but Gwen nudged him. Finally he choked out his line: "By Grabthar's hammer, what a savings!"

A few balloons were released into the air, and then it was time for autographs again.

Finally, Jason made his entrance, as late as usual. But he somehow didn't look himself. There was a twinkle in his eye that made him look disoriented, yet exhilarated.

Spotting his colleagues at the cast table, he quickly headed over toward them. In his haste, he ran smack into Brandon. Brandon and Jason both went down, along with armfuls of *Galaxy Quest* collectibles.

"Commander!" stammered Brandon. "My apologies."

Brandon's friend Kyle nudged him, urging him to say something.

"Commander," began Brandon, "evidently we had some miscommunication regarding yesterday's scheduled voyage, and—"

But Jason, still in a haze, simply gathered his things and walked off.

"He dissed us *again*, Brandon!" spluttered Kyle.

Brandon tried to hide his disappointment. "He probably . . . has some very important business to attend to," he said lamely.

But Hollister, one of the other nerds in the group, was too frustrated to keep quiet. "Maybe we should just start a *Star Trek* club!" he shouted bitterly.

Brandon looked at Hollister with hard, cold eyes. "Don't *ever* say that to me again," he said.

He walked away as the others glared at Hollister.

Over at the autograph table, the actors looked up to see Jason approaching. "Do you know what time it is? Why did you even bother to show up?" Alexander asked bitterly.

Jason tried to speak, but he had so much to say that he couldn't get a word out. Gwen noticed his wrinkled, slept-in clothing and his wild eyes.

"Jason, are you all right?" she asked him.

Jason just pointed to the sky. "*I was there*," he said. "*Up. There.*" The words started tumbling out. "They came to the convention. I thought they were fans, but they're not. They took me up to their ship. They're called Thermians or Thatians, I don't know . . ."

The others exchanged glances as Jason kept talking. "What they built . . . It's incredible! I fought this man, this *thing*, called Sarris. I kicked his *ass*! They have these—pods. One took me through a black hole." he smiled crazily, realizing that they were all staring at him, but not caring. "I know. I know what you're thinking. But I can prove it. Look! They gave me this!"

He searched his pockets frantically, and victoriously produced the interstellar vox, which blinked its little red light.

The others exchanged glances again, then wordlessly produced their own blinking voxes and set them on the table.

"Yes, but can you talk to people in *space* on yours?" said Jason. He spoke into the vox. "*Protector*, this is the Commander. Come in, *Protector* . . ."

Alexander couldn't contain himself any longer. "What a bloody fool," he muttered.

"That's it," said Tommy, rolling up his sleeve in preparation for socking Jason. "It's go time."

"Don't do it, Tommy," said Gwen. "He's not worth it."

Looking down, Jason noticed a label on his vox, which read "Property of Brandon Wheeger." Aha! That was it. "This isn't mine. Where's that kid?"

"You know," said Gwen, "it's one thing to treat us this way, but how can you do this to your fans?"

But Jason was now looking at something else. Standing before him was Laliari, the Thermian crew member. She was flanked by two young crewmen.

Fred glanced at her casually, then turned back for a harder look as her exotic beauty sunk in.

"Begging your pardon, Commander," said Laliari. "We come with news. Sarris lives. He was able, upon your departure, to make an escape. However, he has contacted us and wishes to surrender. We humbly implore you to return with us, to negotiate the terms."

Jason turned to the others. "They want me back," he gushed. "You have to come with me. It'll be the most amazing experience of your lives. We're going to negotiate an alien general's *surrender* in *space*. You have to— guys? Guys?"

But they had already begun to walk away, one by one, in disgust. Only Gwen remained. She looked at Jason.

"Gwen, you know me," said Jason. "I'm a lot of things, but I'm not crazy."

But Gwen just shook her head and walked off.

So there it was. Jason would go alone.

Standing before a mirror in the store's stockroom, he

inspected himself. He meticulously smoothed his commander's insignia and carefully picked a piece of lint off his shirt. He looked into his own eyes for a long moment. Nearby, a pod disk on the floor glowed.

"I'm ready," he said.

The actors entered the small office that was serving as their dressing room. "You should have let me hit him," Tommy said to Gwen.

"I don't know, guys," she said. "I mean, he almost looked . . . *sincere*."

Fred looked thoughtful. "I think we should have taken the gig," he said. "Who knows the next time he'll ask us."

They all turned slowly to Fred as the meaning of his words sank in. "Of course," said Tommy. "He was talking about a *gig*. A *job*!"

In moments, the actors were hurrying through the aisles of the store. They spotted Guy, who was talking to a fan.

"Commander come through here?" Gwen interrupted.

"Yeah, come on," Guy responded, leading them toward the back of the store.

Laliari was still in the stockroom, alone, when they got there. She lit up with happiness as they entered.

"We're coming too," said Gwen.

"Wonderful!" said Laliari. "The Commander had me

continue transmitting, in the hopes you would change your mind." She spoke into her vox. "*Protector*, requesting five interstellar pods for immediate departure."

Tommy rolled his eyes at Gwen. "These fans . . ." he muttered.

But Gwen suddenly noticed the pod disks that were glowing beneath their feet.

"Guys?" she said. "Guys?"

"I look forward to meeting you all in person when we arrive at the ship," said Laliari. "End transmission."

And with that, Laliari blinked and vanished. She had simply been a hologram transmission.

The full realization of the situation was starting to hit Gwen. "Oh, my God," she said. "*Oh, my God.*"

Out in deep space, the pod bay of the *Protector* lit up with a series of brilliant flashes. In rapid succession, the pods were arriving through a hatch in the ceiling, each with its own flash.

The pods unfolded to reveal Gwen, Alexander, Tommy, and Guy, who stood paralyzed. Their teeth chattered.

A metal hatch was in front of them. Beyond it they could hear the sound of wet, squishing footsteps. They were growing closer.

The hatch began to open. Their eyes began to widen.

And then, there they were. Five horrible, tentacled, drooling, screaming alien monsters. They surrounded the visitors, probing them with jagged devices.

Then one of the monsters looked down at a mechanism on his belt. "Oops," he said. "Crewmen, your skins! Activate your e-skins!"

The monsters flipped switches on their belts, and at once their forms became human. They were uniformed as ship's technicians.

"Our most sincere apologies!" said one of the technicians. "We forgot about our appearance generators."

Then Jason appeared in the doorway, wearing a big, warm smile. "Guys!" he said. "You came!"

The actors, however, were not yet in the swing of things. They just stood there, still paralyzed in fear from the sight of the aliens.

"Okay, who wants the grand tour?" offered Jason cheerily.

Guy was now relaxed enough to let out the loudest scream he had ever screamed.

"Okay, Guy," chirped Jason. "Anybody else?"

Abruptly, there was another streak of light, and Fred appeared alongside the others. He stepped off of the disk, completely unaffected by his journey. Nothing got to Fred.

"Now that was a heck of a thing," he said. He looked at the others, and nodded to Jason. "What's wrong with them?"

Jason just smiled and led the group down the hall. They shuffled forward, silent and dumbfounded, staring at their surroundings. Occasional involuntary jerks of their limbs gave evidence of their horrifying journey.

"That's right . . . just keep shaking it out," said Jason. "Here, have some gum, it helps."

"Wh-where are we?" stammered Tommy.

"Twenty-third quadrant of gamma sector," Jason replied, completely the confident Commander. "I can show you on a map."

Then Mathesar appeared, coming down the hall with a small group of aliens. "Welcome, my friends! I am Mathesar. On behalf of my people, I wish to thank you from the deepest place in our hearts." He reached out to shake their hands respectfully. "Dr. Lazarus," he said. "Lieutenant Madison. Young Laredo, how you've grown. Tech Sergeant Chen. And . . ." he looked quizzically at Guy, not sure who he was.

"Crewman Number Six," he said. "Call me Guy."

"You . . . know us?" said Gwen, still shell-shocked.

Mathesar laughed softly. "I don't believe there is a man, woman, or child on my planet who does not," he said. "In the years since we first received your ship's historical documents, we have studied every facet of your missions, technologies, and strategies."

"Historical documents," Alexander repeated, mystified.

"Yes. Eighteen years ago we received transmission of the first. It continued for four years, and then stopped, as mysteriously as it came."

"You've been watching the sho—" said Tommy, but stopped short when he was nudged sharply in the ribs by Jason. "I mean, the historical records, out *here*?"

"Yes," Mathesar said. "Our society had fallen into disarray. Our goals, our values had become scattered. But since the transmission, we have modeled many aspects of our society from your example, and it has saved us. Your courage, teamwork, friendship through the adversity . . ."

They all sneaked looks at each other.

"In fact," Mathesar continued, "all you see around you comes from the lessons garnered from the historical documents."

"*That's* why you built this ship?" Gwen gasped.

"It's incredible," said Guy.

"Oh, this?" said Jason, his eyes twinkling. "This isn't the ship. This is only the starport for the ship. You want to see the ship?" He pushed a button and a door opened, leading to a docking pod.

They entered the pod. The doors slid shut and the transport started moving. It cleared a wall, and the enormous NSEA *Protector* came into view. It was a magnificent and breathtaking sight.

"Oh, my God, it's real," Alexander whispered.

"All this from watching the . . . historical records?" Gwen asked in disbelief.

"Yes," said Mathesar, "and from your supplementary

technical documents, of course." He motioned to another alien, who withdrew a number of brightly colored books and boxes from a backpack.

The actors looked at the material. All of it was familiar to them; they'd seen it a hundred times at the *Galaxy Quest* shows. It was all there: the fan books, the software bearing such titles as "The Official Blueprints: NSEA Protector" and "Virtual *Galaxy Quest*: The CD-ROM Experience."

Tommy began to giggle. Alex looked at him, at the fan stuff, then out at the enormous ship, and he began to laugh too. One by one, the others joined in as they headed toward the giant ship. It was all too unbelievable.

Inside the great ship at last, the group walked down the corridor, peeking into various rooms, more awestruck every second. As they passed each room, the crew members inside saluted.

Walking through the ship, Guy always seemed to be just outside the group, a little late, always trying to see between their heads.

Mathesar was leading the tour. "Weapons storage," he said. "We have eight hundred thirty-eight magneto-pistols, seventy-two vox, and a valence shield for every crewman on board. The medical quarters are to the left. We went to some trouble duplicating your cellular regeneration systems . . ."

Looking past Mathesar, Fred couldn't help notice

Laliari casting a glance in his direction. His heart skipped a beat.

Meanwhile, the others were whispering at Jason: "What the hell is going on?" hissed Tommy.

"Jason, what have you gotten us into?" said Alex.

"I don't believe this, it's insane!" whispered Gwen.

"Calm down, everybody," said Jason. "We're just here to negotiate General Sarris's surrender."

"'*Just*'?" said Alexander.

Mathesar did not notice the conversation his guests were having. ". . . the organ fabrication chamber is coming along nicely. The maintenance facility . . . the dining hall . . ."

"Jason, this is crazy!" said Gwen. "We should get out of here!"

"You want to go home?" Jason asked Gwen. "Fine. Say the word, and we'll all go home and feed the fish and pay the bills and fall asleep with the TV on and miss out on *this*. Is that really what you want?"

There was silence. Clearly nobody wanted to miss this.

Mathesar was still going. "We have enjoyed preparing some of your more esoteric dishes. Your 'Monte Cristo' sandwich is a current favorite among the adventurous. The main barracks . . ."

Two hundred crewmen rose to attention as the group passed. Jason saluted back. "At ease, men," he told them.

As they moved on, Alex muttered under his breath.

"Like throwing gasoline on a fire," he said. Then he turned to Guy, who was grinning from ear to ear.

"What are you smiling for?" Alexander asked.

"I'm just jazzed to be on the show, man!" Guy responded excitedly.

Finally, they arrived at the generator room. In the center was a large orb, pulsating with light. When it dimmed, it appeared to have a rocky texture, like a large boulder. Many technicians were scurrying about, tending to the measurement devices that surrounded the orb.

"Our beryllium sphere, of course," said Mathesar. "I hope, Tech Sergeant Chen, that this meets with your approval."

Fred ran his finger along a gleaming copper tube. "Fine," he said. "Real clean."

Three younger crewmen approached Mathesar, whispering. Then Mathesar hesitantly approached Fred. "Tech Sergeant Chen," he said, "I am sorry to ask this of you so shortly after your arrival, but members of our reactor staff have a question they find most pressing."

"Uh-huh?" said the affable Fred.

"Sir," said one of the young techs, "we have had unexplained proton surges in our delta unit. They cannot be verified on the subfrequency spectrum but appear on the valence detector when scanning the beryllium sphere. We are unable to resolve this problem and were hoping you would be able to advise us."

Silence. Everyone turned to Fred.

"Well," said Fred, hedging, "that's a puzzler, isn't it?"

Fred turned to one of the techs. "Uh . . . what do you think?"

"That possibly . . . the valence bonds have shifted bilaterally?" the tech answered nervously.

"What does that mean?" Fred asked.

"What does that mean? Yes, I see! Yes . . . it means that perhaps—the bonding molecules have become covalent?!"

"Covalent," said Fred, rubbing his chin wisely. "Right. So . . . ?"

"So our solution is to introduce a bonding substrate and bombard the ions with their reflective isotopes!"

"Okay!" said Fred happily.

The other techs grinned, astonished. "Of course!" said one of them. "It's so obvious! Sergeant Chen, you're—a genius!"

Fred modestly waved off the praise.

"Now," said the grateful Mathesar to the actors, "I suggest that you rest before we take the ship out of dock. These crewmen will escort you to your quarters."

In the media room, Tommy's escort, Neru, handed Tommy his weapons. "Here is your valence shield. Your vox. Your magneto-pistol. We know you prefer a sensitive trigger," he added.

Tommy grinned at the display.

"Is there anything else you require?" Neru asked.

"Uh, no, I'm good," Tommy told him. "Here you go," he added, slipping a few bills into Neru's hand.

With a perplexed look, Neru looked at the tip, then made for the exit.

Meanwhile, Alex's young escort, Quellek, led him down the hall. "Dr. Lazarus," he said haltingly, "I hope that I'm not breaching protocol, but—I am so very humbled to stand in your presence. Though I am Thermian, I have lived my life by *your* philosophy, by the code of the Mak'tar."

"Well, good, that's very . . . nice," said Alexander.

"By Grabthar's hammer, Dr. Lazarus," said Quellek emotionally, "I—"

Alex cringed at the sound of the infernal catch phrase. "Don't do that. I'm not kidding."

"I'm sorry, sir, I was only—"

"Just don't," barked Alex.

"Yes, sir," Quellek replied, crestfallen.

They came to a stop in front of a door. "Your quarters, sir." Quellek opened the door. The room was a gray square, completely barren.

"This is it?" said Alexander.

"Yes, sir. Marvelous, isn't it? Completely distraction-less."

"Where's my bed?"

Quellek pushed a button, and six large spikes rose from the floor. "Just as on your home planet, sir. If I may say, it took me three years to master the spikes, but now I sleep with a peace I never thought possible."

"Is that the bathroom?" asked Alexander, full of dread.

"Yes, sir," replied Quellek proudly, leading him in. "The use of your waste facilities were strangely absent from the historical records, so we had to extrapolate purely on the basis of your anatomy."

Alex looked down at a thing that looked more like a torture device than a toilet, with elaborate tubes and stirrups and plugs going everywhere.

"You're quite complicated, sir," said Quellek earnestly.

Alex stared at the thing in despair.

Gwen was changing into her *Galaxy Quest* uniform in her cabin, which was an exotic and beautiful room, when she heard a knock on the door.

"It's Jason."

"One minute," Gwen called. "I'm dressing."

He came in. "Oh come on, it's not like I haven't—"

They just looked at each other for a moment, and then Gwen broke out into a smile, trying to find the words.

"Yeah, I know," said Jason.

"I just can't believe it," she said. "Any of it! Look at this room! They designed it based on the Tuaran pleasure ship from 'historical document' thirty-seven. Oh, and listen to this," she added. "Computer?"

"Yes?" replied the computer's voice.

"What's the weather like outside?" Gwen asked.

"There is no weather in space," said the computer.

Gwen giggled. "I never get tired of that joke."

"Let me try," said Jason. "Computer?"

No response.

"Computer?"

"Only answers to me," Gwen said, smirking.

"But I'm the Commander!"

"On the show I talk to the computer and repeat what it says," Gwen explained. "So that's what they built."

"C'mon," said Jason, changing the subject. "We're wanted up on the command deck."

"Wait. When are you going to tell them?"

"Tell them? About what?"

"Who we are. Don't you think they're going to be kind of mad?"

"Are you kidding?" said Jason. "I'm not going to tell them."

"Jason, you have to tell them. What if something happens? We're *actors*, not astronauts. We can't do this stuff!"

"It's not the *stuff*. Anybody can learn the *stuff*," he said. "The important thing is *commitment*. Ninety-nine percent of anything is just committing to it."

"Ninety-nine percent of *acting* is commitment. *Acting*. Your acting teacher never manned a resonance cannon, she taught *acting*!"

Gwen moved toward the door.

"Hey . . . hey, where are you going?" said Jason.

"We have no right to do this," she replied. "They deserve to know."

"Gwen, no, wait!"

Just then the door opened, and in came Laliari carrying a glowing pad. "Lieutenant Madison," she said, "the females of the ship have requested your hand imprint for the proposed Tawny Madison Institute for Computer Research."

Gwen's eyes softened as she pressed her hand into the pad. "The Tawny Madison *Institute*," she said dreamily.

Jason smiled. He knew he had her.

"Well," said Gwen to Jason, in the same dreamy voice, "maybe we could stay a *little* longer . . ."

On the way to the command deck, Jason and Gwen

met up with Tommy, Alexander, and Guy. "What's going on?" Tommy asked.

"I think we're going to exit the spaceport," Jason said.

When they reached the familiar command deck, they stood and gawked, waiting for the show to start. They didn't quite realize that they *were* the show.

"If you would all take your positions," Mathesar prompted them.

The actors jumped. "Oh, right . . . *us!* Yes, of course. *Us!*"

They took their positions at the familiar-looking control panels.

"Look at this," Tommy said, turning to Guy. "I remember I had it all worked out. This was forward . . ."

"You know where my console is?" Guy asked, only half listening to Tommy.

"Your console?" Tommy responded incredulously. "You don't have a console. You're just Crewman Number Six."

Dejectedly, Guy wandered off to find a place to settle. Along the way, he bumped against a simple flashing-light panel, revealing an intricate matrix of technology underneath. He tried to fit the panel back into place before anyone noticed, but Mathesar was right behind him.

"As you see," Mathesar said, snapping the low-tech panel back on, "we had to use some of our own humble neural biological technology to simulate your far more advanced systems."

"Hey, that's cool," Guy told him, his casual tone hiding his awe.

Mathesar turned toward Jason. "Commander," said Mathesar, "some of the crew has requested to be present at this historic event." A few crew members entered, followed by a dozen more, and then fifty more. They stood around the edges of the room, watching eagerly.

Tommy turned to Guy. "No pressure, huh?" He chuckled. "Glad I'm not the Commander."

"Okay, Laredo, take her out," said the Commander.

Every pair of eyes in the room turned toward Tommy. His sarcastic smile disappeared instantly. "Excuse me?" he said.

"They designed the ship from watching *you*," Jason reminded him. "So . . . take her out, Lieutenant."

Tommy stared down at his control panel, panic-stricken. It was pretty self-explanatory, just a throttle and a circular dial for direction. But it was daunting nonetheless. "Right," he muttered to himself. "Okay, yeah, sure."

Every eye remained glued to him as he nudged the throttle forward gently. The engines rumbled to life, a massive, exhilarating sound. Tommy giggled nervously. His hand trembled as he pushed the throttle further. The ship started to move.

"Oh, God," chanted Tommy. "Oh, my God . . ."

The giant craft eased heavily forward, sliding through the sides of the dock. Nobody breathed. Tommy turned the navigation dial slowly as Guy whispered directions to him: "More to the left . . . Stay parallel . . ."

"Hey, *you* want to drive?" Tommy finally snapped at him.

But Guy was right, the ship was off course. It was like trying to get out of a tight parking space with concrete walls to either side. But much, much harder. The ship was veering ever so slightly into one of the walls.

Tommy turned the dial to correct the ship's angle. The bow of the ship moved closer and closer to the wall.

And then, there was the sound of a soft but high pitched *scraaaaaaaape*. The ship stopped, grazing the wall ever so slightly.

"Uh-oh," said Tommy. He grasped the throttle and moved it forward again, just a bit. *Scraaaaaaape*. He kept going, in too deep to back out now. The ship continued to *scraaaaape* for a couple of horrible seconds as it completed the curve, and then—it was free. The beautiful craft glided slowly out to open space, with only a few scratches on the paint job to show for the incident.

Jason and the others let out a sigh of relief. "Very good, Lieutenant. Forward, Mark Two," he said, giving the command he'd given a zillion times on the show.

Tommy smiled, just as relieved. He pushed the throttle to the 2. "Mark Two, Commander," he repeated.

At dinnertime, the actors and their new alien friends

sat around a large table in the mess hall, eating an extravagant meal. Mathesar proposed a toast. "To our brave guests," he said. "Few in this universe have the opportunity to meet their heroes. We are blessed to count ourselves among them."

Jason waxed poetic for the occasion. "Wherever a distress signal sounds among the stars, we'll be there, this fine ship, this fine crew. Never give up, never surrender!"

Everyone clinked glasses.

Teb turned to Tommy. "We are sorry about the instrumentation, Lieutenant Laredo," he said. "There must have been a malfunction in the steerage mechanism."

"Just see that it doesn't happen again," said Tommy sternly.

"Yes, sir," said Teb.

He turned to Gwen. "How are you enjoying your food, Lieutenant Madison?"

"Oh, it's fantastic. French is my favorite," she replied.

"Yes, we programmed the food synthesizer for each of you, based on the regional menu of your birthplace." Teb now turned to Alexander. "Are you enjoying your Kepmok bloodticks, Dr. Lazarus?" he inquired.

Alexander was toying miserably with a bowl of live insects that were swimming in a disgusting, vomit-textured broth. "Just like mother used to make," he managed to say before pushing the bowl away, nauseated.

Dinner went on and on, course after course. Jason

entertained his captive audience.

"The beast *roared* as I *plunged* the knife again and again," he declaimed. "I held on for dear life as it thrashed about! That was the day I learned that a Klive serpent bleeds red." He looked around dramatically. "What price man?" he asked. "What price man?"

Alexander ignored him, as always. "Tell me, Mathesar, this Sarris bloke we're flying to meet," he said. "What is it he wants exactly?"

"For years," Mathesar explained, "Sarris has plundered the resources of our planet. We built this ship in order to find a new planet to settle—one far away from Sarris. We are not accustomed to confrontation. We are scientists. This ship was to be our salvation."

A tick jumped off of Alexander's spoon and back into the soup.

"But Sarris found out about our plans just as we had completed construction of the *Protector II*," Mathesar continued. "He heard about the device—the Omega 13."

"The Omega 13," mused Guy. "Why does that sound so familiar?"

"The lost footage," Gwen told him. "At the convention. The mysterious device in our last episo—I mean *historical document*."

"What is it? What does it do?" Tommy asked.

"We don't know," Mathesar replied.

"But—you built one, right?" Gwen asked.

"We built . . . something," Teb explained, "from the

blueprints and what references we could find on your Internet. But there is much about the device that we don't even understand. We were hoping you could enlighten us."

Jason tried to rise to the occasion. "Well, it's . . . This was a device we—er—discovered on an alien planet." He looked around at the others for help. None came. "We don't know what it does either," he admitted lamely.

"Why don't you just turn it on and see?" Tommy suggested.

Teb shook his head. "It has at its heart a reactor capable of generating unthinkable energy. If we were mistaken by even the slightest calculation, the device would act as a molecular explosive, causing a chain reaction that would obliterate all matter in the universe."

"Mathesar?" said Jason. "Has Sarris seen the, er, historical records?"

"No, thank God he has not."

"Then how did he find out about the device?" Jason asked.

"Our former commander was not . . . strong," said Mathesar sadly.

"Former commander?" Jason echoed.

"I'm sorry," said Mathesar. "You deserve to be shown." He nodded to a crewman, who pushed a button. A wall slid back to reveal a large viewscreen. An image appeared on the screen, but it was full of static, and the sound cut in and out.

"The tape was partially demagnetized as it was

smuggled off of Sarris's ship," Mathesar explained.

The earthlings watched as an image emerged from the static. It was the former commander, in his alien form, strapped to a metal board. Each of his wrists and ankles was secured with mechanical devices and twisted in different directions.

"Originally, one of our own tried to lead," Mathesar choked.

On the screen, Sarris stood over the alien, holding a control panel. "Is that all?" Sarris was hissing. "You have no more to confess to me? After three days of this you still require incentive?" Sarris moved a switch on the panel, and the device pulled at the alien's limbs, twisting them horribly.

"I have told you all I know!" cried the alien commander. "To my shame, I have told you everything. If you have any mercy within you, please, let me die!"

"Oh, I shall, I shall." Sarris smiled. "When I grow weary of the noises you make, my little plaything, be assured, you shall die." He toyed with his control panel.

Mercifully, the screen fuzzed up with static.

The earthlings' mouths hung open in horror. Jason stared, the blood draining from his face as he realized that the current commander was—him.

Dinner was over. The actors hustled down the hallway behind Jason, panicked.

"We're leaving, Jason," said Gwen. "We're leaving *now*."

"Let me think. I need time to think," said Jason.

Tommy chimed in. "There's nothing to think about!"

"Listen," said Guy, almost hysterical. "I'm not even supposed to *be* here. I'm expendable. I'm the guy who dies to prove that the situation is serious!"

Before Jason could speak, Mathesar came running up, looking distressed. "Commander," he said.

Jason cut him off. "Mathesar, I need you to prepare pods for my crew," he said.

"Your crew? What about you?" asked Gwen.

Jason looked torn.

"Begging your Commander's pardon, sir," said Mathesar, "but we cannot launch pods at the moment. Sarris will surely detonate any objects leaving the ship."

Jason stared at him, not quite comprehending.

"Yes, sir, he is here *now*. Your presence is required on the command deck."

Alarmed, they all sprinted up to the command deck.

"There's nobody here, Jason," said Gwen.

"Mathesar," Jason said, "maybe we should get some of your crew up here."

"I thank you for your consideration to our pride," said Mathesar, "but while my people are talented scientists, our attempts to operate our own technologies under tactical simulation have been disastrous."

The actors were going to have to run the ship.

Mathesar leaned over to where Gwen sat at the computer station, and pushed a button. "I have raised Sarris on zeta frequency," he said.

"Uh . . . great. Thanks," she said numbly.

Jason tried again, feeling desperate. "Still, Mathesar, your crew may nonetheless be helpful in certain—"

But he was interrupted by the sight of Sarris, who appeared on the large viewscreen. Sarris now wore a metal eyepatch and had a long scar across his cheek.

"We meet again, Commander," said Sarris.

The crew stared at Sarris.

"Hi, Sarris," said Jason, looking as nonchalant as possible. "How are you doing?"

"Better than my lieutenant. He failed to activate ships's neutron armor as quickly as I'd hoped on our last encounter." He lifted a stake into view. The head of his lieutenant was impaled on it.

"Right," Jason dithered, panicking. "Well—listen, I'm, I'm sorry about that whole, um, *thing* before." He tried a laugh. "I'm sure we can work this out." He motioned to Sarris's eyepatch. "That going to heal up? I feel just awful about that."

"Deliver the device now or I will destroy your ship," was Sarris's reply.

"Listen, I'd like to," said Jason, "but frankly, I'm not sure where it is, or even—"

"You have ten seconds."

"All right. You got it. You win. I'll deliver it now. Just give me a moment to set it up." Jason was thinking madly.

He made the finger-across-the-throat gesture to Gwen, signaling her to cut the transmission. She nodded.

"All right," he said, "nobody panic, I've dealt with this guy before and believe me, he's as stupid as he is ugly."

"Jason . . ." said Gwen urgently.

"We're going to fire everything we've got at him, all right?" said Jason.

"*Jason* . . ." she repeated.

But Jason was too juiced up to listen. "You just keep pushing those buttons and send everything at him, okay?"

Guy looked at the buttons labeled with icons of armaments. "Okay," he said doubtfully.

"All right," said Jason. "Put me back on with Sarris."

"I've been trying to tell you," said Gwen. "You *are* on with him."

"Perhaps I am not as stupid as I am ugly, Commander," commented Sarris.

Jason turned to Gwen, horrified. "I made the '*Cut the*

line' gesture. You nodded okay!"

"I thought it was the 'We're dead' gesture! I was agreeing!"

"Listen, Sarris," said Jason in a nervously jovial sort of way, "you can't blame me for trying."

"Of course not," said Sarris.

But their conversation was interrupted by Guy. "Guys!" he said. "Red thingy moving toward green thingy. Red thingy moving toward green thingy!"

"What?" said Jason.

Guy motioned toward the radar screen, where a red blip was about to impact a green one.

"I think we're the green thingy," said Guy.

"A present for you, Commander," said Sarris.

"Turn!" shrieked Jason. "Gun it! Get out of—"

But there was no time. The ship was pounded by a torpedo blast. Unlike on the the TV show, which involved a lot of running back and forth and shaking the camera whenever they were "hit," this was the real thing. The entire crew went flying across the cabin and into the walls. The lights flickered.

For the first time, they felt genuine fear. They weren't acting anymore. This was *real*.

Another blast hurled them into the walls like rag dolls.

"We've gotta get out of here!" cried Jason.

Tommy looked at the sparkling map of lights on his dash.

The "peculiar fans" from the planet Theramin.

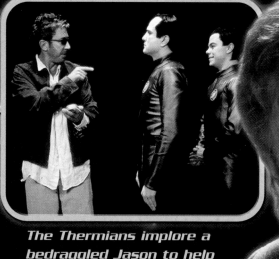

The Thermians implore a
bedraggled Jason to help
save them from enemy
forces.

Jason Nesmith
as Captain Peter Quincy Taggart

Face-to-face with a Thermian—
in his true form.

The crew aboard the
NSEA Protector.

Tommy Webber
as Navigator and Gunner
Lieutenant Laredo

Gwen DeMarco
as Shipmate Tawny Madison

The evil *Sarris*

Sarris with a Thermian prisoner.

The Thermian leader greets his
guests at a formal dinner.

Fred Kwan
as Tech Sergeant Chen

To save the ship, the crew must locate a new beryllium sphere on a nearby planet.

Alexander Dane
as Dr. Lazarus of Tev'Meck

Jason goes head-to-head with a vicious pig lizard.

Back on the ship, the "Captain" is captured.

Mathesar is tortured by Sarris's men.

Jason and his crewmates defend the ship from the enemy invasion.

"Just *go*! *Go! Punch go!*"

Tommy punched the red button, and they all held on for dear life as the ship roared forward, across the path of Sarris's ship.

"They're turning!" Gwen screamed. "They're *coming!*"

An explosion rocked the ship, then another, and another.

Above the din, the computer's even voice could be heard. "The ship is sustaining structural damage," it said.

Gwen did her usual job. "Guys, we're sustaining structural damage!"

"Faster, Tommy. Get us out of here!" yelled Jason.

Tommy cranked the dial. "It's as far as it goes!" he said.

"They're still behind us," Guy fretted.

"We should have a turbo booster," said Jason. "I'm always saying 'Activate turbo boosters,' right?"

"Could be this," said Tommy, finding a new button.

"Push it. Hold it down," Jason ordered.

Tommy pushed the turbo button. The ship began to vibrate.

"The enemy is matching velocity," warned the computer.

"The enemy is matching velocity," warned Gwen.

Suddenly an image appeared on the side viewscreen. It was Fred, down in the generator room. He was taking it all in stride.

"Hi, guys," he said. "Listen, they're telling me that the

generators won't take it, the ship's breaking apart and all that. Just FYI." Then the viewscreen went black.

The ship roared forward.

"We've got to stop!" said Alexander.

"We stop, we die," said Jason. "Keep holding the thruster down, Tommy!"

"You don't hold a thruster down!" Alexander argued. "It's for quick boosts!"

Jason gave him a look. "Like *you* know?" he said.

The ship groaned and creaked, and then a loud, honking siren sounded.

Gwen froze. "I remember that sound!" she said. "That's a *bad* sound!"

Jason looked forward. A sort of shapeless mass could be seen in the distance. "Maybe we can lose them in that cloud," he said.

Gwen peered at it. "I don't think that's a cloud."

She was right, of course. It was nothing as simple as a cloud. As they approached, they began to see that the cloud was actually made of thousands upon thousands of slowly rotating cubes.

"Mathesar? What is that?" Jason asked.

"It's the Tothian mine field, left standing from the great war of 12185," Mathesar told him.

"Mines? Oh, lovely!" said Alexander, his voice dripping with sarcasm.

"The ships are gaining," said Gwen.

"Do your best, Tommy," Jason urged him.

But it was too late. They were in it already. The first mine hit, rocking the ship. Tommy swerved to avoid it, running into another mine, and then another. He couldn't have done worse if he'd been aiming at them.

"They're drifting toward me!" Tommy said. "I think they're magnetic!"

The ship hurtled forward through the mine field, suffering considerable damage as the mines impacted.

Inside the enemy ship, the *Falcon*, Sarris calmly watched the *Protector* fly into the almost certain death of the mine field.

"Continue forward, sir?" asked Lathe, Sarris's eager lieutenant.

"Patience, Lieutenant," said Sarris. "Patience."

Back on the *Protector*, things were going from bad to worse. The ship was vibrating horribly. It groaned and creaked. Rivets started to pop, sending deadly projectiles flying every which way.

"We're almost through," Tommy said through gritted teeth. "Come on . . . hold . . ."

Everyone was yelling at once.

"We have to stop!" screamed Alexander.

"Front armor is gone!" Gwen shouted. "Just slow it down a little!"

"No!" Jason yelled. "We're almost through!"

"Don't be insane. Stop! Full stop!" Alexander hollered at Tommy.

"Keep going! Keep going!" Jason hollered even louder.

Tommy was a wreck. *"What do I do? What do I do?"*

There was a loud grinding noise. Then silence. The vibrating stopped. Gwen looked up from her radar screen.

"What's happened?" said Alexander.

"The engines are dead," Tommy said. "We're drifting."

"Are they behind us?" Jason asked Gwen.

"No, I don't think so," she replied. "Wait. They're not,

but . . . *something* is." She looked harder at her rear view-screen. "Oh, my God."

They all looked, just in time to see two dozen magnetic mines, bearing down on them in a cluster.

"*Down!*" yelled Jason.

They barely had time to brace themselves as the ship was rocked by waves of explosions. There was nothing to do but hit the floor and try to ride it out.

As the last of the mines exploded the ship was sent tumbling lifelessly through space.

From the outside, the ship looked dead. The exterior lights were dark. The once-shiny hull was now blackened and ragged.

Inside, too, the deck looked devoid of life. The lights were dim. The sirens had stopped, and it was completely silent. The crew slowly emerged from behind panels and equipment, their faces sooty, their clothing torn and bloody.

Jason moved to Gwen. "Are you all right?" he said in a choked voice.

She nodded, and began pulling herself to her feet. "Tommy," she said. "Where's Tommy?"

They heard a groan. Tommy was crumpled against the wall, his arm twisted impossibly. He was in agony. "It's broken," he moaned. "Oh, God . . ."

"I'll take him to medical quarters," said Betzalar, the ship's medic.

Next Alexander rose, blood trickling down his forehead. "Go into the cloud!" he quoted Jason mockingly.

"Alex? Where are you going?" said Gwen as he headed for the door.

"To see if there's a pub."

A short while later, the battered crew regrouped in the ship's strategy room. Alexander nursed a blue beverage as Tommy examined a high-tech metallic cast on his arm. They were listening to the computer's assessment of the damage.

". . . Forward thruster shaft, 87 percent damage. Left vector guards, 96 percent damage. Level 5 structural breaches in quadrants 32, 34, 40, 43, 58 . . ." intoned the machine.

"And the engines?" Jason asked it.

"Computer, what about our engines?" Gwen repeated. "Why don't we have power?"

"The beryllium sphere has fractured under stress," reported the computer.

"It's fractured," Gwen repeated hopelessly.

"Can it be repaired?" Jason asked.

"Computer, can it be repaired?" said Gwen.

"Negative," replied the computer. "The beryllium sphere must be replaced."

"We need another one," said Gwen.

"Oh, boy," said Guy. "The beryllium sphere. That's bad."

Despite his blue drink, Alexander lost it. "You broke

the ship!" he screamed at Jason. "You broke the bloody
ship! I told you you don't hold down a turbo. You push it
once, maybe twice—for a *boost*! You don't *hold* it!"

Jason ignored the outburst. "Do we have a replacement beryllium sphere onboard?" he asked.

"Computer," said Gwen, "do we have a replacement
beryllium sphere onboard?"

"Negative, no reserve beryllium sphere exists onboard."

"No, we don't have an extra beryllium sphere," Gwen
repeated.

"You know," said Tommy, "that's really getting
annoying."

Gwen turned on him. "Listen," she said, in a low and
deadly voice. "I have *one* job on this lousy ship. One job.
It's stupid, but I'm going to *do* it. *Got it?*"

"Sure, no problem," said Tommy, backing away.

Suddenly the door opened, and in came seven
Thermians, led by Mathesar.

"A thousand apologies," said Mathesar. "We have
failed you."

Jason was the first to speak. "You what? What are you
talking about?"

Mathesar was distraught. "We have seen you victori-
ous in many more desperate situations," he said. "The
fault must lie with us, with the ship."

Gwen shot Jason a glance. *Tell them*, she said wordlessly.

Jason could no longer stand it. "No . . . Listen, Mathesar," he said. "It's not your fault. We're—we're—uh . . ." but he petered out, too chicken to finish.

Gwen took control. "We're not the people you think we are," she said.

Mathesar looked confused. "I don't understand."

Alexander tried another tack. "Mathesar," he said, "don't you have television on your planet? Theater? Films?"

Now Mathesar nodded, relieved that he was understanding. "The historical documents of your culture," he said. "Yes, in fact we have begun to document our own history, from your example."

"No," said Gwen, "not historical documents. I mean—surely you don't think *Gilligan's Island* is a—"

Mathesar and the others looked sad. "Those poor people." He sighed.

"Hoo boy," said Tommy. This was going to be way hard.

Gwen was determined. "Does no one on your planet behave in a way that is contrary to reality?" she said.

"Ah," said Mathesar. "You speak of . . ." unable to bring the words to mind, he conferred with his fellows. "Deception," he said finally. "Lies."

"Well, sort of . . ." said Jason.

"We have become aware of these concepts recently," said Mathesar. "In our dealings with Sarris. Sarris will say one thing and do another. Promise us mercy and deliver destruction. It is a concept we are beginning to learn at some great cost. But if you are saying that any of you could have traits in common with Sarris . . ."

He started to laugh, and the other aliens joined in. "You are our Protectors—our heroes. You will save us."

Suddenly Fred, still down in the generator room, appeared on the viewscreen.

"Hey, Commander," said Fred. "We found some beryllium on a nearby planet. We might be able to get there if we reconfigure the solar matrix in parallel for endothermic propulsion. What do you think?"

"I—well, uh . . ." Jason stammered, unable to respond. Then he regained his composure. "Yes, absolutely!"

Fred turned to the two young techs next to him. "Gold star for you and gold star for you," he said, beaming.

Soon the ship began to lumber forward, and in a little while the swirling globe of a colorful and mysterious planet was visible in the forward viewscreen.

The group had gathered near a small surface pod. Quellek stepped forward and handed Alex a device. "Dr. Lazarus," he said, "here is your surface mapper. I have programmed it to the coordinates of a beryllium sphere of sufficient density.

"Good luck on your mission, sir," said Quellek emotionally. "By Grabthar's hammer, by the suns of Warvan, I wish you—"

Alexander held up a warning finger. "Uh-uh," he

chided. "What did we talk about?"

"Right. Sorry, sir."

Laliari turned toward Fred, holding out a small locket. "For luck," she told him.

Fred took the locket and, smiling, boarded the pod after his fellow crewmates.

With Tommy at the helm, the pod approached the planet. Guy looked out the window nervously. "I changed my mind," he said. "I want to go back."

"After the big fuss you made about not getting left behind on the ship?" asked Alexander.

"Yeah, but that's when I thought I was the crewman that stays on the ship and something kills me, but now I'm thinking I'm the guy who gets killed by some monster five minutes after we land on the planet."

"Guy," said Jason, "you're *not* going to get killed, okay?"

Guy was getting more and more agitated. "Oh, I'm not? I'm not? Then what's my last name?"

Jason was perplexed. "Your last name?"

"Yeah, what is it?"

"It's . . . I don't know."

"No. Nobody does. Do you know *why*? Because my character isn't *important* enough for a last name. Because I'm going to *die* in five minutes, so why bother to come up with a last name for me?"

"Guy," said Gwen reasonably, "you *have* a last name. We just don't *know* it."

"Do I? *Do* I? For all you know I'm just 'Crewman Number Six'! Guy was getting hysterical again. "It's *Fleegman*! Guy *Fleegman*! There! *They can't kill me now, can they? Can they?*"

Finally, Jason slapped him.

"See?" Guy went on. "I'm the hysterical guy who needs to be slapped, and then I die!"

"Are we there yet?" Alexander sighed.

The pod made its way toward the surface of the planet, and landed, shaking just enough to make everyone anxious. After they'd set down, everyone applauded, complimenting Tommy on the landing. Tommy averted his eyes, ashamed.

"Autopilot," he mumbled.

They heard the *whoosh* of the airlock on the hatch decompressing. Fred grabbed the handle to open it.

"What are you *doing*? Don't *any* of you watch the show?" Guy screamed. "You don't just open the door! It's an alien planet! Is there air!? *You don't know, do you?*"

But they had no choice. Fred opened the hatch, and sniffed the air. "Seems okay," he said, shrugging.

Tentatively, they exited the craft. Alexander looked down at his mapper. "This way," he said. They all turned. "Wait, no, that way . . ."

"You were holding it upside down, weren't you?" Tommy asked.

"Shut up," said Alexander.

"All right, let's all settle down," said Jason. "If we're going to get through this, we're going to have to exercise self-control."

"Self-control. That's funny coming from you," muttered Gwen.

"Did it ever occur to you that if you had been a little more supportive you could have held on to me?" Jason said to her.

"I could have held on to *you*!"

"We're really going to do this *here*?" said Alexander.

But they weren't going to do it there. The landscape was too menacing.

"How much further?" Jason asked.

Alexander measured the distance on the device between his fingers and held them up. "About this much," he said.

"What's the scale?" Jason asked. "Ten miles? A hundred miles?"

"*This* much," Alex repeated, showing him.

Guy, meanwhile, was casting his eyes around, a look of dread on his face. "Something's wrong . . . There's something wrong here," he was saying.

He looked over his shoulder to at the rocky trench they had just passed through. There was indeed something wrong there, but it was hard to figure out exactly what it was. Somehow, the rock shapes in the path behind them seemed vaguely like arms and hands, reaching out of the landscape.

They climbed crest of the hill, with Guy bringing up the rear.

Suddenly, Guy yelled. The others turned to see him on the ground, his foot lodged in a crevice.

He screamed hysterically. "It's got me! It's got me! See? *Five minutes!*"

"Easy, son, it's just your imagination," Jason told him, clapping Guy's shoulder in a commanderly way.

"You're playing your good side," Gwen noted.

"Don't be ridiculous," Jason told her.

But the others were playing along now. "Note the sucked-in gut," Alex put in.

"And the sleeves rolled halfway up the biceps," Tommy added.

"It's the rugged pose," Fred summarized.

The others nodded in agreement as Guy hopped up

and down, trying to get his shoe back on.

Suddenly they heard a noise. Spooky alien whispering, it sounded like. And critters climbing around on the surrounding cliffs.

Guy threw up his hands. "That's it, that's what's going to kill me."

Below them, they could see a small, abandoned mining facility. Wind whistled through the various structures and power stations. In the center of the outpost sat a large, shimmering boulder.

"There's the beryllium sphere," said Alexander.

"Where is everybody?" asked Gwen.

Guy shivered. "Something *bad* happened here."

Suddenly they became aware of a small blue creature emerging from one of the structures. It looked somewhat like a human child. It moved to a small pool of water and began drinking. Its movements were very quiet and tentative.

Then a few more blue children emerged and join the first one.

Gwen smiled, amazed. "Will you look at that," she said. "They look like little children."

"We should get out of here," said Guy.

"Wait," said Gwen. "Look." Another blue creature had emerged. This one limped, as if its leg was hurt. It moved forward, dragging its bad foot along the ground, making noise.

The blue children didn't seem to like the noise. They turned their heads and began whispering in an alien tongue.

"Gorignak," whispered the alien children. "Gorignak . . . nak nak!"

Gwen smiled. "Aw, look, they're going to help the hurt one. They're so cute!"

And indeed, the others were moving toward the hurt creature, cocking their heads to the side empathetically.

"They're cute now," said Guy. "But in a second there are going to be a million *more* of them and they're going to turn *mean* and *ugly* . . ."

Right on cue, two dozen more blue children emerged, surrounding the hurt one. They smiled with sharp razor teeth, their mouths spreading out impossibly on their faces. They descended on Limpy, closing in on him. In seconds, there was nothing much left of him.

The earthlings were silent.

"I am so sick of being right," said Guy at last.

Jason took a deep breath. "All right, here's the plan," he said. "First, Fred, we need a diversion to clear those things out of the compound. Then Gwen, Alex, Fred, and I go down to get the sphere. Any of those kids starts coming back, give a signal. Guy, you set up a perimeter."

"Why does this sound so familiar?" asked Gwen.

"'Assault on Voltareck 3,'" said Tommy. "Episode—Thirty-one, I think."

"We're doing Episode Thirty-one?" said Guy quickly.

"Whatever," said Tommy, "the one with the hologram. How the heck is Fred supposed to project a *hologram*?"

"Jason, *are we doing Episode Thirty-one? Are we?*" asked Guy in a panic.

"It's a rough plan, Guy! What does it matter if we're doing Episode Thirty-one or not?" said Jason.

"*Because I died in Episode Thirty-one!*" shrieked Guy.

Alexander interrupted his cries. "This is ludicrous," he said, gesturing toward Jason. "Why are you listening to this man? Must I remind you that he is wearing a costume, not a uniform? He's no more equipped to lead us than *this* fellow," he said, motioning toward Guy. Looking at Guy he added, "No offense."

"You have a better plan, Alex?" said Tommy.

"As a matter of fact, I do. Look at their eyes. They're obviously nocturnal. Come sundown they will go into the forest to hunt. So we simply to wait for the nightfall instead of mounting an insane assault in full daylight simply because we did it that way in Episode Thirty-one!"

Two hours later, the sun was setting. As the last glow sank into the horizon, everyone rose to begin the assault.

They had just started forward when the second sun—the *big* one—rose up behind them, lighting the planet brightly.

The actors turned to Alexander, who looked away

sheepishly. Jason smiled and stood up, vindicated.

"So. As I was saying . . . Fred, we need some sort of diversion," he directed.

"Right, the hologram," Fred offered, sounding unsure.

But when they looked down, it seemed that the blue demons had already deserted the complex. "They must have gone back inside," Gwen said.

Jason was in full Commander mode now. "Okay, Gwen, Alex, Fred, follow me. Guy, set up the perimeter. Tommy, you keep a lookout, and make a signal if they come back."

"What kind of signal?"

"Anything."

"Okay," said Tommy, "I'll do this." He cupped his hands over his mouth. "Caw, caw!" he went ridiculously.

"Tommy," said Jason, holding up his vox, "we have these."

"Oh, right, sorry."

"Okay, let's go."

The group started down the hillside, leaving Tommy and Guy to stand guard. Heading down the ridge, Jason was in full action mode, using the dramatic commando tactics he'd used on the show. He ducked behind a rock, peeked out, then rolled on the ground to the next rock. Gwen, Alex, and Guy just strolled down casually behind him.

"How does the rolling help, actually?" Gwen asked him.

"It helps," Jason replied with feeling.

Gwen stared at him for a moment. "Where's your gun?" she asked.

Jason slapped his hip, hoping to find the gun there. But it was gone, lost during one of his dramatic rolls.

"It helps," Alexander commented sarcastically.

The abandoned compound was spooky. A battered metal door swayed and creaked in the wind. They passed a metal console with a number of broken viewscreens. One, however, was partially intact. Fred pushed a button, and it lit up.

They watched, aghast, as a blurry scene of mayhem played back on the video screen. They could see a number of alien miners running frantically through the compound. Thunderous crashes, like gigantic footsteps, could be heard. A terrified miner, face wrapped in cloth except for the eyes, stared into the camera, mumbling. He was out of his mind with fear. "Gorignak . . . Gorignak," he said.

The image went blank. The actors looked at each other.

"Anybody want to wait around to find out what a Gorignak is?" said Jason.

They all shook their heads.

"Let's do this," said Jason grimly.

Up on the ridge, Tommy looked down on the compound with his binoculars. He could see Jason and the others moving toward the beryllium sphere. He scanned the compound. Good, no blue children.

Guy was still agitated. "I know what it is," he babbled, though nobody was listening. "I know what it is. It's not what's *on* the planet. It *is* the planet."

Tommy moved the binoculars back and forth between Jason and the others at the sphere, and the deserted complex. He could see them start to roll the sphere. It moved forward with a rumble.

A blue hand emerged from one of the structures. Tommy frowned.

Guy was still going. "There's a life force here. The blue things—did you see how they moved? Careful. Quiet. Like they didn't want something disturbed . . ."

Up above, Tommy could see demon children emerging from the mining structures. "Uh-oh," he said.

Oblivious, Jason and the others strained to roll the boulder up the incline. "C'mon, push!" Jason urged. "Never give up, never surrender!"

"Oh, shut up!" the others replied in unison.

Suddenly they all froze. They had noticed the returning demons. The monsters gathered around them, forming a vicious circle of slavering teeth. There was silence.

And then Tommy's voice, loud and clear on the vox: "Caw! Caw!"

Alexander sighed.

Suddenly, a series of magneto-pistol blasts rang out,

melting pieces of equipment and putting holes in the walkways. The aliens scattered for cover.

Gwen and the others turned to see Tommy coming, the gun in his hand, followed by Guy.

"Sorry, guys. It just went off," he apologized.

"Good work, Tommy," said Jason. "Let's go!"

Grunting, they pushed the sphere over the lip of the incline. It started to roll on its own, faster, and faster still, until Jason and the others were running to keep up with it.

Jason looked over his shoulder, and then turned forward. "Don't look back," he shouted to the others, his voice earnest. "Do not look back."

But Gwen couldn't resist. She looked back, and there they were: hundreds of blue demons coming over the hillside like a tidal wave.

They had almost reached the surface pod. Moving as fast as they could, they started to push it up the entrance ramp. But the boulder was too big. It blocked the door.

Gwen helped Guy inside, then squeezed through herself, followed by Tommy. Alexander and Jason were left outside.

"Go ahead!" Alexander shouted to Jason.

"You go first!" returned Jason. "There's no time!"

"Oh, of course, I forgot!" Alexander said. "You have to be the hero, don't you? Heaven forbid I get the spotlight once! Oh no, Jason Nesmith couldn't possibly—"

Jason clocked him, knocking him unconscious, and lifted him inside. Then he started to squeeze through himself.

"Tommy, I'm in, push *GO* now!" he panted.

But Tommy was a second too late. Five pairs of demon hands grabbed Jason by the ankle and dragged him back outside. The door closed behind him.

"Oh, my God!" Gwen shrieked. "Tommy! Stop the pod! Stop the pod!"

"I can't," wailed Tommy helplessly. "It's on autopilot!"

As the pod ascended, they all moved to the window to watch, horrified, as Jason disappeared into the huge blue mob that surrounded him.

Alexander regained consciousness and joined the others in looking down at the scene below.

"Oh, of course, Jason," he muttered bitterly. "It's always about *you*, isn't it?"

Back on the planet's surface, Jason was surrounded by the menacing demons. They stared down at him with their chilling smiles. Then they leaned in, their mouths opening for the kill.

Suddenly, a shadow washed over them. A blue demon looked up over his shoulder, terrified. "Gorignak," he whispered meekly.

9

The surface pod returned to the ship carrying Gwen, Alexander and the others. As soon as the pod bay doors opened, they rushed out into the generator room. Teb and three other technicians were waiting for them.

"We got the sphere," panted Gwen, "but the Commander's down there with a bunch of cannibals!"

"Teb, reset the pod, we're going back," said Fred.

Tommy shook his head. "That thing's not going to get us down there fast enough. Face it, he's dead."

"Wait, Fred," said Gwen. "What about that thing—you know, 'Digitize me, Sergeant Chen!'"

"The digital conveyor," said Fred.

"Of course!" said Guy excitedly. "We'll just zap him up with the digital conveyor!"

Tommy turned to Teb. "Do we have one of those?" he asked.

Teb nodded, and led they way as they all sprinted down the hallway after him.

As they ran, Alexander caught up with Gwen. "You said 'the Commander,'" he puffed.

"What?"

"Back there. You said, 'The Commander is down there with a bunch of cannibals.'"

"No I didn't."

"Yes you did."

"Is this really the most important thing we could be talking about right now?" said Gwen irritably.

On the planet's surface, Jason lay unconscious on the ground. He was awakened by a snort. Opening his eyes, he found a large beast, grunting and nudging his shoulder. It looked like an oversized, somewhat reptilian sort of pig.

From above, along the rock walls, Jason could hear the sound of the blue demons whispering: "Gorignak . . . Gorignak . . ."

He scrambled to his feet and reached for his gun, but it was gone. He needed a weapon, any weapon. Quickly, he removed his shirt and snapped it at the beast, trying to drive it away. But the beast kept trying to chomp at him, holding its ground.

Suddenly, Gwen's voice sounded: "Jason? Can you hear me?"

"Yes! Yes, I'm here!" he shouted, grabbing his vox.

"Thank God," said Gwen. "Are you okay?"

"Yeah. But I've got Gorignak staring me in the face. I think I can take it, though."

"Jason," said Gwen, "we're going to use the digital conveyer to get you out of there."

Jason swiped at the pig lizard. It hissed at him petulantly. "The digital conveyer?" he said. "You mean I'm going to get diced into cubes and sorted up there in a thousand pieces?"

"Right," said Fred pleasantly.

Jason thought about it. "I'll take my chances with Gorignak," he said. The pig lizard nipped at him, and he threw a rock at it.

"Jason, we've got to get you out of there," said Gwen. "It's perfectly safe, isn't it, Teb?"

"It has never been successfully tested," Teb admitted.

Jason strained to hear this conversation. "What? What did he say?"

"Nothing," said Gwen. "Hold please." She switched off the vox and turned to Teb.

"Theoretically," Teb explained, "the mechanism is fully operational. However, it was built to accommodate your anatomy, not ours. But now that Sergeant Chen is here, he can operate it."

Everyone turned to Fred. For the first time, he looked a little apprehensive. He laughed nervously. "Well, I mean, I can't . . . I can *supervise*, of course, but—"

Alexander now got on the vox to the Commander. "Jason, we're going to test it," he said.

"Okay . . ." said Jason slowly. "On what?"

"How about the pig lizard?" Tommy suggested.

"Hey, I was doing okay with the pig lizard," Jason protested.

But the plan was already in motion. Alexander and

the others watched on the viewscreen as Fred manned the control panel. The controls fit Fred's hand like metal gloves.

Teb gasped. "I'm sorry," he said. "It is very exciting to see the master at the controls. The operation of the conveyer is more art than science."

Fred moved his hands, targeting the creature in the crosshairs of the instrument panel. He slowly, cautiously twisted his wrist, and . . .

Poof. On the planet's surface, Jason gaped as the pig lizard digitized and disappeared.

Fred smiled as the creature rematerialized on the platform. No sweat, this digital conveying.

But something was very wrong.

Down below, Jason could hear the thing's horrible squeals over the vox, and the disgusted reactions of the crew. "What? What?" he cried in alarm.

"Nothing," said Alexander in a singsong voice.

Beside him, Teb was upset. "But—the animal is inside out," he said.

"I heard that!" Jason yelled. "It's *inside out*!"

The next sound he heard was a sort of wet exploding sound.

". . . and it exploded!" added Teb.

"What?" said Jason. "Did I just hear that it came back *inside out*, and then it *exploded*? Hello?"

"Hold please," said Gwen.

Behind Jason, unseen demons were still chanting.

"Gorignak . . . Gorignak . . ."

"Wait," Jason said into the vox. "The pig lizard is gone. Why are they still chanting?"

"Turn on the translation circuit," said Gwen to Teb.

Teb flicked a switch. Now the demons could be heard chanting in English. "Rock . . . Rock . . . Rock . . ."

Gwen and the others noticed that the entire rock face behind Jason was moving slightly, like muscles made of granite.

Gwen spoke cautiously into the vox. "Jason? I don't think the pig lizard was Gorignak."

"What are you *talking* about?" said Jason.

The boulders in the wall began moving forward, and something emerged from the rock face. It was a monster made of granite. As he heard the rumbling sound of the monster freeing itself from the rock, Jason turned slowly. A cold feeling of dread was wrapping itself around him. "Oh my God," he said.

He took a step back. The rock monster headed straight for him, its featureless face oddly ominous.

Jason had a bad, bad feeling. "Guys, digitize me," he said into the vox. He backed away slowly, but the monster followed. *Crunch . . . crunch . . . crunch . . .*

"Guys . . . ?" said Jason.

Up in the digital conveyer room, Fred was sweating. "C'mon, Fred," Gwen encouraged him. "They based it on *your* hand movements."

Fred looked at their expectant faces. "Didn't you see what happened?" he asked. "What is *wrong* with you? He is going to *die. Why are you all looking at me?!*"

Down below, Jason was in a full-out run. At his heels, the rock monster stomped forward, demolishing everything in its path.

Then he heard Alexander's voice on his vox. "Fred's no good, Jason," it said. "You're going to have to kill it."

"*Kill it?* Well, I'm open to ideas!"

"Go for the eyes," said Tommy. "Like in Episode Twenty-two with—"

"It doesn't *have* eyes!" Jason shrieked into the vox.

"The throat, the mouth," Tommy tried. "Its vulnerable spots."

"It's a rock. It doesn't have vulnerable spots!"

The monster's huge shadow fell over Jason. "Alexander?" he tried. "Please? You're my advisor, advise me!"

"Hmmm," said Alexander. "Well, you have to figure out what it wants. What's its motivation?"

"It's a stupid rock monster!" Jason yelled. "It doesn't have motivation! *Actors* have motivation!"

"That's your problem," Alexander replied testily. "You were never serious about the craft."

Alexander switched his vox on and placed it on the table in front of him. Then he closed his eyes and went into the acting exercise he had practiced a million times before: "I'm a rock . . . I just want to be a rock . . . Still.

Peaceful. Tranquil . . ." He spoke to Jason softly, completely into the excercise. "Oh, but what's this? Something's making noise . . . No, not noise, no . . . *Movement. Vibrations.* Make the vibrations stop, they go straight into me like a knife! I must crush the thing that makes the vibrations . . ."

Somewhere around the middle of this monologue, Jason's eyes lit up. "Am I crazy," he said, "or do you actually have something there?"

Hesitantly, Jason reached down and scooped up a handful of small rocks.

But he was a moment too late, for the rock monster chose that second to reach down and grab him in its fist. Thinking fast, he tossed one of the rocks at a nearby overhang. This dislodged a few more rocks, which tumbled noisily to the ground.

The rock monster turned toward the sound, dropping Jason as it did so. Alex was right—the thing hated noise! As soon as he hit the ground, Jason threw another rock, making as much noise as he could.

The monster charged toward the wall. *CRUNCH!* The overhang, unable to take the impact, fell apart. Down came an avalanche of rock, burying the monster. Up in the ship, a cheer went up.

But the celebration would have to wait. As Jason stared, the rocky rubble was re-forming itself. A newer, *bigger* monster was taking shape.

Before Jason could react, the thing was making a bee-line for him.

But I'm not moving, he thought. Then he stopped short. He'd figured it out. His heartbeat. The thing couldn't stand the thumping.

"Fred," he called into the vox. "You've got to do this. It's up to you."

"No, Jason, I'll mess it up!" cried the terrified actor.

"Listen, Fred," said Jason. "You did this for four years on the show. You can do it now. Put your hands on the controls."

Fred put his trembling hands on the controls. Sweat poured down his temple. He muttered nervously. "That was the show. I'm not that guy."

The monster was now picking up speed, stomping rockily toward Jason.

"I knew a Fred Kwan who never went up on a line. I knew a Fred Kwan who never missed his mark."

"That's not me anymore, man," Fred replied dejectedly.

"It is, Fred," Jason told him. "You just stopped trying. Now, you're going to do this. You're going to save my life."

"I am?" Fred answered, starting to believe in himself.

"No doubt in my mind," Jason told him. Behind him, the monster raised its fist.

"*Digitize me, Fred!*"

And then, as everybody held their breath—as the monster smashed its fist right down onto Jason—Jason digitized. The fist went right through the scattering blocks that had been Jason.

And then, there he was on the platform, his body still contorted to duck the monster. As he regained his composure, everyone came running over, hugging him, patting him on the back. Even Alexander looked relieved, though he wouldn't admit it. "I see you managed to get your shirt off," he said, smiling.

Jason looked over to see Fred still at the controls, drenched. He went to him and shook his trembling hand.

"Welcome back, Fred."

Fred's eyes welled with pride. He turned toward Laliari, and a look passed between them. But the moment was broken by the sound of Jason's voice.

"All right! We've got the beryllium sphere hooked up?" he asked.

"Back to full power," Teb informed him.

"Pods and engines?"

"Fully operational," Laliari responded.

"Okay!" he called out. "Raise the command deck, Teb. You can drop us off and still get back to your planet in time for supper."

Teb looked perplexed. "Oh no. We have no reason to go back," he told Jason. "We are all that is left."

Jason stood for a moment, unsure of what to say. Then Teb spoke again.

"I have raised the command deck."

Jason spoke into his vox. "Mathesar, we're on our way to the command deck. Mathesar? Come in, Mathesar? Teb? Quellek? What's going on? Where is everybody?"

Gwen pushed a button on one of the monitors. Sarris's ship was outside.

Gwen punched another button, and more video panels lit up. Sarris's men were all over the ship. In the generator room, the hallways, the command deck. It was an infestation.

"We've got to get out of here," said Jason. "C'mon, hurry!"

But as they headed toward the door, it opened, revealing Sarris and a dozen of his men, guns drawn. The actors backed away, except for Jason, who stood his ground as Sarris approached.

"Listen, Sarris," he began. "Just hold on—"

Sarris backhanded Jason brutally, crashing him to the floor. With a nod from Sarris, six of his men surrounded Jason and began to kick and beat him.

In a few moments, it was over. Jason, bloody and beaten, was led down a long hallway, followed by Sarris, his guards, and the other crew members. The row of barracks had been converted to prison cells. Hundreds of aliens watched in despair as Jason, weak and semiconscious from the beating, stumbled and fell. Sarris applied a device to Jason's neck. Jason cried out as his entire body convulsed.

"If you cannot walk, Commander," said Sarris coldly, "then I suggest you crawl."

The medical deck had been converted to an interrogation chamber, into which Jason was led with the others. Sarris's men were already at work, interrogating a man strapped to a table. It was Mathesar, barely alive.

But when he saw Jason, a ray of hope lit up behind his eyes. He smiled. "Commander," he whispered. "Thank God you're alive." He turned his face toward Sarris. "Now you will face justice," he said.

Sarris just laughed. "At every turn," he said, "you demonstrate the necessity for your extermination. The qualities of your species . . . ridiculous optimism, like little children." He turned to Jason. "Do you wish to save this man's life, Commander?" he asked. "And the life of your crew?"

"Yes," Jason replied, barely audible.

"Then tell me one thing: What does it do, the device? The Omega 13."

"I . . . I don't know."

Sarris twisted a dial, and Mathesar writhed in pain on the table.

"Is it a bomb?" Sarris asked Jason. "A booby trap? Tell me!"

"Stop, please! I don't know!" cried Jason.

"Prepare a harness for the female," Sarris directed.

"No! I swear I don't know! Please!"

"Do you think I'm a fool? That the Commander does not know every bolt, every weld of his ship?"

Gwen fought the guards valiantly as they dragged her to a table.

"But I'm not! I . . . I'm not the Commander!" wailed Jason.

Sarris turned, interested. He motioned his guards to halt. "Wait. What did you say?"

"Please," said Jason, "don't hurt them, it's not their fault. I'm not the Commander, I don't know anything."

From his table, Mathesar looked at him, bewildered.

"Explain," said Sarris.

Jason turned to Gwen. "The show," he said. "There's no choice. Do it."

All eyes were on Gwen. Sarris was intrigued by this new development. "Computer," she said, "play the historical records."

A screen lighted up, showing the opening of the first *Galaxy Quest* episode. The actors were all in their roles, freeze-framed in action poses.

Sarris watched, captivated. Slowly, realization dawned on his face. He began to laugh. "Oh, this is wonderful," he said to Jason. "Wonderful. I treated you as a foe, but no—you have done greater damage to these poor fools than I ever could have. Bravo! Bravo!"

He put his arm around Jason and led him over to Mathesar. "Tell him," he said. "This is a moment I will treasure. Explain who you really are."

Jason took a deep breath, hardly able face Mathesar. Finally he began to explain. "My name is Jason Nesmith," he said. "I'm an actor. We're all actors."

"He doesn't understand," said Sarris. "Explain as you would to a child."

Jason tried again. "We pretend," he told Mathesar. "We—we lie."

"Yes . . ." Sarris grinned. He was loving this. "You understand *that*, don't you, Mathesar?"

Mathesar looked up at Jason, bewildered.

Jason bowed his head. "I'm not a commander, there

is no National Space Exploration Administration. There is no ship."

Mathesar, totally perplexed, pointed to the monitor. "But there it is!"

"A model," Jason said, "only as big as this." He showed Mathesar with his hands.

"But . . . inside, I have seen—"

"Sections of rooms made of plywood. Our beryllium sphere was painted wire and plaster. It's all a fake. I'm not him." He looked over at Gwen. "I'm a nothing. A nobody."

"But . . . *why?*" asked the stricken Mathesar.

Jason shook his head slowly. "It's difficult to . . . On our planet, we pretend in order to . . . entertain."

Mathesar just stared at him, as Sarris watched, eyes twinkling.

"That's how I make my living," Jason went on sadly. "Pretending to be somebody else. Pretending to be Commander Peter Quincy Taggart. I'm—I'm so sorry, Mathesar."

Mathesar looked away, his eyes hollow, all hope gone.

"Now you know," said Sarris gleefully. "This entire world you've concocted. All based on nothing. Your beliefs—your hopes. All a dream. Now there is only pain."

Sarris moved to his lieutenant, Rak Lathe. "Lieutenant Lathe," he said, "I confess I am beginning to feel a bit foolish myself. Chasing across the universe to obtain what is, I am now certain, a bauble of fiction. How can we obliterate this vessel? I would like nothing to remain."

"The core could be hardwired to overload without much effort," said Lathe.

"What about my men?" Mathesar asked Sarris.

"Yes, you're right. Much too easy a death for the trouble you have caused me. Lieutenant, open a vent on level C and let the outside in a bit for our friends."

There was a moment of shocked silence. Then, an enraged Jason lunged for Sarris. But he was no match for Sarris's men. They quickly beat him down.

"I guess an actor is not the same as a commander after all," Sarris chuckled.

He turned to his guard, motioning to Jason and the others. "Release them, Sergeant," he said, bored now. "Into space."

The guard nodded and began to escort them out. As they were leaving, Sarris turned to Mathesar and twisted the torture control with a sick smile.

They were marched to the nearest airlock. As they walked, they could hear the computer's voice reverberating throughout the ship. "Core overload," it warned. "Emergency shutdown overridden. Core implosion estimated in nine minutes . . ."

One of the guards pushed a button, and the airlock door opened with a whoosh. "You two. Go," he said to Jason and Alex.

They started toward the airlock. Jason hung his head.

"Get in," ordered the other guard. "Hurry up." He hustled them into the airlock.

Jason turned to Alex with a steely glare. "What the heck are you looking at?" he snapped.

Alex just stared back, perplexed.

"I said what are you looking at, you fin-headed monstrosity?" Jason cried.

Alexander continued to stare. Then he realized what Jason was doing. "You murdered us all," he said, playing along.

"Shut up," Jason told him.

"How does it feel? Hundreds will die because of you," Alex went on.

"Shut up!" Jason exploded. "Just shut up!"

Alexander lunged at Jason, striking him in the face, and they tumbled outside of the airlock, fighting. The guards smiled, enjoying the fight. Jason quickly overpowered Alexander and punched him repeatedly, his anger taking hold. They locked in a mutual stranglehold. Then Jason pulled free. He grabbed Alex by the collar and pulled back for the crowning blow . . .

And dealt a punisher, right past Alexander and into the face of the first guard.

Alexander turned, realizing it was all an act. He flashed Jason a smile and elbowed the other guard in the face. The guard's gun skittered into the airlock as he dropped to the deck, unconscious.

The first guard dived into the airlock. He grabbed the gun and aimed at Jason. But suddenly the inner door snapped shut. An instant later, the outer door opened. Gunshots ricocheted against the glass as he was whisked into space, flailing silently in the vacuum.

"A bit sticky," said Fred, taking his finger off the air-lock button. "I'll get one of my boys up here with a can of WD-40."

Alexander turned to Jason. They were both out of breath.

"'Fin-headed monstrosity?'" he said to Jason.

Jason shrugged. "I was staying in character."

"I see you got to win the fight," Alex added.

"I had the shot," said Jason modestly.

"Guys . . ." Gwen interrupted. She pointed to a row of security monitors. On one of them four of Sarris's men were straining at a large circular valve. On another monitor, they could see debris rushing up to a vent, as air was sucked out of the barracks where the aliens were imprisoned. Teb and the other aliens were pulling on their prison bars in terror.

"Let's go," said Jason.

They ran down the hallway, ducking into an alcove as a unit of Sarris's men jogged past.

The computer voice was still echoing through the ship: "Core implosion in four minutes . . ."

Jason looked at Gwen. "Go on, give it a try," he said.

Gwen took a breath and then said, "Computer, shut down the core."

"Unable," replied the computer voice. "Memory checks invalid. Core systems hardware damaged."

"All right, guys," said Jason, making up a plan as he went along. "Uh—Gwen and I are going to shut down the core manually. Fred, you and Guy need to get that air valve back on. Alex, see if you can get the prison doors open downstairs."

"Jason? What about me?" said Tommy. "What do I do?"

"Practice driving, Tommy."

Gwen and Jason hurried down the hallway. "So," said Gwen, "we get to shut down the neutron reactor?"

"Right."

"Uh—I hate to break it to you, Jason, but I don't know how to shut down a neutron reactor. And unless you took a Learning Annex course I don't know about, I'm pretty sure you don't know how to shut down a neutron reactor either."

"No, I don't. But I know somebody who does."

Outside Brandon Wheeger's house in southern California, birds were chirping pleasantly. It was a sunny Earth day.

Brandon was sitting at his computer, wearing his *Galaxy Quest* uniform, gluing a tiny piece of plastic to his model of the *Protector*.

There was a knock on his half-open door. "Brandon? The garbage, honey?" Mrs. Wheeger called.

"Mother," said Brandon testily, "I'm quite busy, as you can see. The C rings on my booster unit came broken in the mail."

"C'mon, Brandon. Don't make me ask again."

"Ten more minutes," he promised.

Brandon looked at his model with a sigh. Suddenly he heard a familiar tone. It was the interstellar vox, sitting on his table. "What the—?"

Slowly he reached out and flipped the switch.

"Hello? . . . Hello, is anyone there?" it said.

Brandon stared at the thing, then looked around his room for signs of a practical joke. Finally he spoke into it, quietly, because he felt like a jerk. "Hello?"

"This is Jason Nesmith. I play Commander Peter Quincy Taggart of the NSEA *Protector*."

Brandon stared at the vox for a very long moment. "Yes?" he finally said.

"We accidentally traded vox units when we bumped into each other on Saturday," said Jason's voice.

"Oh, I see." Brandon was on his guard. His last encounter with Jason Nesmith had not been very pleasant.

"Brandon, I remember you from the convention, right? You had a lot of little technical observations about the ship, and I spoke sharply to you . . ."

"Yes, I know, and I want you to know I thought about what you said. I know you meant it constructively, but—"

"It's okay. Listen—"

"But I want you to know that I am not a complete braincase, okay?" said Brandon. "I understand completely that it's just a TV show. There is no ship, there is no beryllium sphere, no digital conveyor. I mean, obviously—"

"It's *real*, Brandon. All of it, it's *real*."

"I knew it!" yelled Brandon without a second's hesitation. "I *knew* it!"

"Brandon," said Jason, "the crew and I are in trouble and we need your help."

On the ship, things were looking bad. In the medical quarters, Sarris stood over an unconscious Mathesar, savoring his victory. On a nearby viewscreen he could watch the prisoners in their cells, pulling at the bars.

His first lieutenant, Lathe, approached him. "General, your transport is ready for departure."

Meanwhile, in the media room, Tommy was looking for something. He pushed a button and a panel slid aside, revealing a complete library of *Galaxy Quest* episodes. Moving his finger across the selections, he picked one in particular. He smiled.

In another part of the ship, Alexander was stealthily making his way down the hall, avoiding Sarris's guards. He jumped at a noise from a utility compartment beside him. Steeling his nerve, he opened the door, and a figure jumped out.

Both of them tensed, ready for battle. Then Alexander relaxed. It was only Quellek, his young admirer.

"Sir, it's you! Thank Ipthar!" said Quellek, beaming.

"Quellek! What are you doing in there?"

"I avoided capture using the Mak'tar stealth haze. Where is everyone?"

"Come with me," said Alexander. "I'll explain on the way."

Jason was still on the vox with Brandon. "Okay," he said. "We're in C deck, hallway five. What now?"

In his room, Brandon inserted a *Galaxy Quest* CD-ROM, labeled "Technical Systems," into his computer. A couple of clicks of the mouse, and a three-dimensional diagram of the ship appeared. "Okay, there's a hatch on the port wall," he said, scrutinizing the image. "It leads to a system of utility corridors."

Up in the ship's storage bay, Jason searched in vain. "There's no hatch! There's no hatch!" he said frantically.

"Wait," said Gwen. "Jason, here!" She pushed a concealed button, and the hatch slid open.

Jason breathed again. "Okay, we got it," he told Brandon.

"Okay, you can go on in," Brandon said. "I'm going to get Kyle. He knows the utility tunnel system better than anybody alive."

Brandon punched some keys on his computer, and Kyle popped up in a little window on the screen.

"Hi, Brandon," said Kyle.

"No time for pleasantries, Kyle. We have a level-five emergency. The Commander needs us to get him to the core and shut it down before it overloads."

"Oh, okay," said Kyle. Nothing to it.

"You've got the utility systems walkthrough, right?" Brandon asked him.

"I have sectors one through twenty-eight," Kyle said. "I think Hector has the upper levels."

"We'd better get everybody online," said Brandon. "And Kyle, stop downloading those pictures. You know which ones I mean. The ones of Tawny that you like so much. Your frame rate is unacceptable."

"I'm not downloading pictures!" But Brandon heard the

click of the cancel button, and Kyle's frame rate improved.

In another part of the ship, Fred and Guy were making their way down the corridor marked Sectors 30–50. "Okay," said Fred. "Sector thirty-eight . . . thirty-nine . . . forty. This is it. The environmental systems are in here. All we have to do is shut off the valve to the barracks."

They looked through the window into the room. A hundred of Sarris's men were inside, surrounding the large wheel that controlled the valve. Fred exchanged a look with Guy. *Yeah*, *right*, they were both thinking.

In the media room, Tommy sat at the desk, watching an episode of *Galaxy Quest* play on the screen. The scene featured young Laredo piloting the ship, dodging and weaving around giant a papier-mâché monster that was floating in space. But Tommy was dead serious. He watched himself, mimicking his own piloting moves. "Pedal to the metal, Commander," said both Tommys together.

Jason and Gwen were now running through the utility tunnel system, with Brandon guiding them on the vox.

"Now make a right, you'll see a doorway that opens on the central manufacturing facility," Brandon directed them.

Gwen and Jason turned right. Their eyes widened. Elevators and conveyor belts moved through a maze of scaffolding and overhangs. Glowing rivers of molten metal ran past giant swinging hammers, robot arms, and crushing machines.

"Commander," said Brandon, "do you have a camera? I'd die to see this in person. All they showed on TV was a machine here, and a wall here—I don't know why they didn't show the whole thing."

"We'd never have the budget for this," said Jason, awestruck.

"Okay," said Brandon, back to business. "Do you see a door marked Core Unit?" It should be down at the far end to your left."

On the other side of the room, down a winding path through a dangerous gauntlet of machinery, Jason spotted the door.

"That's where you want to be," said Brandon.

In the corridor outside the barracks, Alexander and Quellek looked through the window at the prison area. Many of the aliens were already unconscious. Others had valiantly attempted to open their cells with crudely constructed levers and battering rams, but to no avail.

Alex tried the door. It wouldn't budge. He looked around and spotted a large computer console. "Here," he said to Quellek. "Help me tear this down. We can use it as a battering ram."

Meanwhile, back at the environmental systems room, Sarris's men still surrounded the main valve.

"We've got to get that valve turned off," said Fred. "Their oxygen is almost gone."

"Listen," said Guy. "I'll go in and create a distraction. I have this." He held up the gun. "I may be able to hold them back long enough for the aliens to escape."

"It's suicide!"

"I'm just a glorified extra, Fred. I'm a dead man anyway. If I'm going to die, I'd rather go out a hero than a coward."

"Maybe you're the plucky comic relief, Guy. You ever think of that?" said Fred.

Guy paused for a moment, and Fred patted his shoulder. "Besides," Fred added, "I just had a really interesting idea."

Sarris stood at the observation window of his ship.

Next to him, the transport chief received a message. "Sir," he reported to Sarris, "I have just received word that the Commander of the *Protector* and his crew have escaped custody."

"*What?*" Sarris's eyes lighted with fury. "Find them," he said, turning to his lieutenant.

Lathe spoke up. "But, sir, my men. The core implosion is not reversible—"

"*Find them.*"

In the bowels of the ship, Jason and Gwen made their

way along a narrow catwalk. Behind them, a row of robot arms moved erratically.

"Okay, Brandon, we're coming up on a six-way intersection." Jason said into the vox. "Now what?"

Brandon had his whole crew on separate windows of his computer screen, including their fellow fan Katelyn, who wore a Tawny Madison outfit.

"All right, you should be at the level seven interchange," Brandon told them. "Enter the circular passage to your left."

Jason and Gwen made their way into the tunnel, then screamed.

"There will be a drop," Brandon added.

"Thanks for the heads up," Jason responded sarcastically.

Jason and Gwen moved forward carefully, inching their way across a narrow beam.

"Commander," Brandon's voice cut in. "What I'd give to see what you're seeing."

"What are you talking about?" Jason asked.

"You're in deep in the underbelly of the Omega 13! It must be spectacular!"

"Doesn't look like much to me," Gwen told him. "Just a few walls and that dumb spinning fan we had in every episode . . ." Her voice trailed off as she followed Jason's gaze and stared upward, awestruck.

"Wow," she said.

After a moment, Jason spoke. "Brandon," said Jason, taking a teetering step, "just in case I die, there's something I have to know."

"Yes, Commander?"

"What does the Omega 13 do?"

"Yes, this is a fiercely debated topic on the newsgroups," Brandon replied. "Most believe that it is a matter *collapser*, a bomb capable of destroying the universe in thirteen seconds. But myself and others are convinced that it is a matter *rearranger*, converting all molecules to their state thirteen seconds prior, thus effecting a thirteen second time jump to the past."

"Thirteen seconds," Gwen commented. "Why thirteen? That's not enough time to do anything of any importance."

"I don't know, Gwen," Jason told her. "There are times I sure could have used one of those. It's a chance to redeem a single mistake."

"But what could you do in thirteen seconds?" she asked him.

"Well," Jason started, sounding hesitant. "You could say 'I love you.' Or 'I'm sorry.'"

"But Brandon," Kyle chimed in, "if all molecules were rearranged, *everyone* would be back in time thirteen seconds . . ."

Suddenly a blast erupted next to Jason's head. He and Gwen spun around to see Sarris's men shooting at them from across the room at the entrance to the cavern.

"Okay—guys? Guys?" Jason said into the vox. He needed advice, and fast.

But the gang was still caught up in the debate.

"No," Katelyn was arguing, "because the brain of the person who triggers the Omega 13 is not affected, so that person still has his memory after the jump."

"Excellent, Katelyn," Brandon said. "High five." Brandon and Katelyn slapped their computer screens.

"*Okay, guys!*" Jason yelled into the vox.

Brandon finally turned his attention back to the problem at hand. "Yes, Commander. All right, you're almost there. Just go through the chompers and over the pit."

"'The chompers'?" echoed Gwen.

The chompers. There they were: an unavoidable gauntlet of hissing, smashing hydraulic hammers and blades. They jutted out from all over, blocking their path in every possible way.

"Brandon," said Jason, watching the horrible metal chompers, "*how?*"

Down on Earth, Brandon cradled the telephone on his shoulder. "Hollister, do you have the sequence yet?" he said.

Hollister was busy watching a tape of the show. He was fast-viewing one sequence over and over, backward and forward. On his TV screen was the cheap, painted-cardboard version of the crushers Gwen and Jason now faced. Hollister timed the pattern of the crushers with a stopwatch.

"Okay," he told Brandon on the phone. "The pattern is two—two—four—two—three—eight—two."

"You're sure? It's sort of extremely important," Brandon said.

Gwen and Jason watched the crushers as they smashed and ground back and forth. "What *is* that thing?" Gwen burst out. "It serves no useful purpose to have a bunch of choppy, crushy things in the middle of a *catwalk*! Why is it here?"

"Because it was on the show!" Jason yelled in exasperation.

"Well, forget it! I'm not going. This episode was badly written!"

"Commander," said Brandon's voice on the vox, "you and Lieutenant Madison will have to go through one at a time, in three-second intervals. Tell me when the first crusher hits the bottom."

Jason waited. "Okay, *now*. But—"

"Wait two seconds then *go*."

Another blast from Sarris's men slammed into the catwalk, weakening it.

"No, wait," said Jason into the vox, "are you—"

"Lieutenant Madison, *go*!" said Brandon.

"Go!" Jason yelled to her.

"*Go*, Commander!" said Brandon.

Jason and Gwen charged through, running for all they were worth. A second's delay would have meant getting crushed by the huge metal parts. Halfway through, a pair of grinding metal teeth snatched at Gwen's sleeve and caught it fast. With a mighty grunt, she used all her strength to pull it loose from the works, a split second before a second hammer came down where her body had been a moment before.

Jason dove through a quickly diminishing hole, his magneto-pistol falling behind him, quickly smashed to oblivion by a closing slab.

"Up," said Brandon.

"What?" said Jason, not sure he'd heard right. "Up?"

"Flame jets," Brandon explained.

Sure enough, there they were. Jason pulled Gwen up just as the flames shot through, sizzling the ends of her hair where it hung down.

"Whoever wrote this episode should die," Gwen spat.

They dropped down and continued on through the doorway, magneto blasts erupting all around them. Suddenly, they were in pitch blackness. "What the hell . . . ? Brandon, where are we?" Jason said into the vox as he ran.

"I don't know," was the reply. "This part of the ship is completely undocumented."

"Great," said Gwen's voice in the blackness. "Just great!"

Alexander and Quellek stood outside the prison area hatch. Through the window they could see the alien prisoners, many of them already unconscious in their cells. Alex tried the door, but to no avail.

"They're dying!" Quellek cried out.

"We have to pry this open a little," Alexander told him, grabbing a makeshift crowbar. "We've got to buy them some time."

"Sir, perhaps if we work together," Quellek began. "With the Mak'tar chant of strength." He looked at Alex and began to chant. "Larak! Tarath! LARAK! TARATH!"

Alexander joined in. "Larak! Tarath! Larak! Tarath!"

After a moment, they heard a *whoosh* and the hatch opened a crack. It wasn't much, but it was enough to hold the oxygen gauge right above "certain death."

Meanwhile, Fred and Guy were in the digital conveyor room with Laliari. Guy and Laliari looked on with great anticipation as Fred gingerly took hold of the controls.

"This should be interesting," said Guy.

On the digital conveyor display, an object was targeted in the cross hairs. The vague outline was that of a man, but blocky and misshapen. It was the rock monster. Laliari smiled, fully grasping Fred's plan.

Down in the environmental systems room, dozens of Sarris's men continued to surround the crucial oxygen valve.

Suddenly, the rock monster materialized behind them. There was a surreal silence for a moment. Then one of the men clicked a button on his transmitter. The rock monster did not like that noise. Not at all.

Laliari turned toward Fred. She looked into his eyes for a moment, then locked him in a passionate kiss. So passionate that Laliari's facial tentacles began to peek out from beneath her hair.

"Uh, okay guys, time to go," Guy called lamely, as Laliari wrapped her tentacles around the back of Fred's head.

On the monitor, the monster chased a group of Sarris's men down a dead-end hallway. It bore down on them, then crashed through the hull, sending the whole group hurtling out into space. The terrified expressions of the men were in stark contrast to the peaceful smile that formed on the face of the rock monster.

Guy and Fred rushed into the now-empty systems room and ran to the large valve, straining to turn it.

Slowly, the pressure normalized.

Alexander and Quellek were now using a battering ram on the door in the barracks hallway.

A readout blinked on Quellek's gauge. "Sir!" he said. "The pressure. It's normalizing!"

At that moment, the door gave way. Alexander burst in, ran to a panel down the hall, and turned the switch. All the cell doors opened. He ran to one of the cells and helped a few of the Thermians to their feet.

They turned to Alexander, gratitude in their faces. "We are saved! He has saved us!" they cried weakly.

Alexander suppressed a smile, preparing to feign modesty.

"Commander Taggart has saved us!"

"It's just not fair." Alexander sighed.

He joined Quellek at the doorway. "Okay," he said, "let's get back to the command deck and—"

Suddenly there was a pistol blast, and Quellek's chest turned red. Alexander and Quellek looked down at the blood, horrified.

Alexander looked up to see one of Sarris's guards running down the hall, still shooting. Grabbing hold of Quellek's limp body, Alexander pulled him to safety.

Quellek opened his eyes weakly, as Alexander checked the wound. It was a mortal injury. Alexander needed to use all of his acting skills to disguise his shock.

"Not so bad," he said, trying not to choke. "We'll get

you to medical quarters. You're going to be fine."

"I—I don't think I'm going to make it, sir . . ."

"Don't talk like that, son. We're going to get you fixed up."

"It has been my greatest honor to serve with you. Living by your example these years, my life has had meaning. I have been blessed. Sir, I . . . I . . ."

He winced in pain. Alexander looked at him, full of emotion. "Don't speak, Quellek," he said.

But Quellek's life was fading away. Alexander stroked Quellek's head, his eyes welling with tears. Then, with absolute sincerity, he said, "Quellek—by Grabthar's hammer, by the suns of Warvan . . . you shall be avenged."

At these words, a tiny spark behind Quellek's eyes lighted up, and he smiled weakly, completely content as he surrendered to death.

Suddenly, a blast hit a nearby corner. Alexander lay Quellek's head to the ground softly, and then rose. There was a new intensity to him. His eyes burned.

Alexander fixed his attention on Sarris's man. The guard looked up, momentarily shaken; Alexander looked truly alien. Nervous, the guard fired twice, missing.

Alexander roared like some enraged creature, baring his teeth as he bore down on the guard. Paralyzed with fear, the guard met his death.

In the substructure, Jason and Gwen were still making their way forward in the darkness. They came to a dead end.

"Brandon, there's a wall," said Jason.

"Oh, good, you should be at the blast tunnel," said Brandon. "Use the computer to open the blast sections in sequence."

"Computer," said Gwen into the darkness, "open the first blast section."

A shaft of light became visible as a huge metal block rose.

They entered a tunnel that ended about six feet in.

"Computer, open the second blast section," Gwen said.

Another enormous block slid up, and the tunnel lengthened.

But now Sarris's men were behind them. Gwen and Jason started running as fast as they could through the tunnel, the blocks rising as Gwen talked fast: "Computer, open blast sections 15,16,17,18,19 . . ."

Finally, they found themselves in a large room with a console in the center.

"Detonation in twenty seconds," said the computer.

"Okay, Brandon," said Jason. "I think this is it."

He moved to a control panel on the console, where he found a blue button.

"How do I shut it down?" he asked.

"Push the blue button," Brandon responded.

"That's it?" Jason said, incredulous.

"What's wrong?" Brandon's voice asked over the vox.

"Nothing," Jason told him. "I just thought it would be more complicated than that."

Jason lifted a clear, hinged flap and was about to hit the button when a volley of shots rang out behind him. Two of Sarris's men appeared in the doorway.

"Raise your hands, now," said one of the guards.

Jason and Gwen raised their hands. In the background, the computer continued its countdown. "Fifteen seconds . . . fourteen . . ."

"Listen, hold on one second while I push this button," Jason said to the guard. "Then we'll talk about whatever—"

That didn't work. They fired a blast and Jason raised his arms again.

"You don't understand!" Gwen yelled. "This ship is going to explode!"

"The general warned us of your tricks," said the guard. He pulled his pistol and leveled it at her.

"This one is strangely attractive," he said, eyeing her lustfully.

"Oh, great," Gwen said, peeved. "This is just *perfect*."

"No, Gar," the other guard told him. "This is sick. It is as if to seek pleasure with an animal."

"Yes, I know," said the first guard.

Gwen had had enough. "You think you can handle me? Do you? Well come on! Both of you! *Come on!*" she cried.

Jason stared at her, incredulous, as the guards took a step toward her. Not a trace of fear showed on her face.

Gwen saw her opportunity. "Computer," she said, "close blast section twenty-nine, please."

The guards didn't even have time to scream as the section block plummeted, crushing the whole lot of them to petroleum in an instant. Goo oozed from under the block.

Gwen turned to Jason. "See? *Nobody* takes me seriously in this outfit," she said. She bent down toward the oozing goo. "Now how are you feeling, *huh*? Do you take me seriously *now*? *DO YOU?*"

As the computer counted down to twelve, Jason flipped up the glass and smashed down on the button. He turned to Gwen with an appreciative smile, and they shared a silent moment. After a beat, Gwen realized that the computer was still counting down.

As the seconds ticked away, Jason punched the button desperately, but to no avail. Anticipating their final moment together, Jason and Gwen embraced. They cringed as the display ticked down to one and . . . stopped.

"It always goes to one on the show!" Gwen and Jason said together.

On the *Protector*, the hundreds of freed Thermians swept through the corridors, overtaking the scattered remnants of Sarris's guards. Alexander fought alongside them, dealing crushing blows to two guards at a time as the aliens swept around him. Alexander and Dr. Lazarus were now one and the same.

Jason and Gwen appeared in the melee. "Alex! Alex, are you okay?" shouted Jason.

Alexander had a faraway look in his eye. "Yes," he said. "Good was done this day."

"Let's go, buddy, they can take it from here," Jason coaxed him. "C'mon." He practically Alex dragged away.

As they ran down the hall, Fred and Guy appeared from around a corner. They all kept running. "Anybody seen Tommy?" asked Jason.

"Right here!" Tommy called, emerging from the media room. He joined them as they sprinted toward the command deck.

"We've got to get the plasma armor up before Sarris finds out we've aborted the detonation!" said Jason.

But it was too late for that. "Warning," said the dis-embodied computer voice. "Enemy missiles launched."

"I think he found out," panted Guy as they ran.

When they reached the command deck, they quickly took their stations. "Forward view!" the Commander commanded.

In the central viewscreen, they could see Sarris's ship dead ahead. A volley of weapons was coming right at them.

"Armor up!" said Jason.

"Plasma armor engaged," Guy responded—just as the ship was rocked by the attack.

"Okay, Tommy," said Jason. "Go! Lose 'em! Into the mines!"

"Into the *mines*?" said Guy.

"Pedal to the metal, Tommy," said Jason with authority.

Tommy drew confidence from the familiar line. "Pedal to the metal!" he repeated. He eased onto the gas and they accelerated—right into the mine field.

Tommy maneuvered with concentration and intensity. Mines whizzed by on all sides.

"Doing good, Tommy," Jason encouraged him. "Real nice."

"Th-thanks," said Tommy shakily.

"You think you could get any closer to those mines?" Jason asked him.

"*Closer?*" Then Tommy smiled, realizing exactly what Jason had in mind. "I can try."

★★★

On the *Falcon*, Lathe was making his report to Sarris. "General, I've lost them," he said. "The magnetism of the field is disrupting our instru— Wait. There they are."

"Get back on their tail," snapped Sarris.

"I can't, sir."

"What? Why not?"

"Because they're coming right at us."

Sarris smiled. "Fire at will," he said.

The *Protector* was rocked by missile blasts, but it held its course—straight for the *Falcon*.

"We're getting hammered, Jason," said Guy. "Return fire?"

"No. Keep all energy to the armor."

As they moved toward Sarris's ship, an image of Sarris appeared on the viewscreen.

"Well, isn't this adorable. The actors have decided to play war with me."

Gwen glanced at Jason. "Sarris's ship is accelerating toward us at Mark Two," she told him.

"Accelerate to Mark Four, Tommy," said Jason.

Sarris kept chatting. "This is embarrassing, really," he said. "I shan't tell this story when I return home."

"He's accelerating to Mark Six," said Gwen.

"Mark Twelve," countered Jason.

The two ships were playing a galactic game of chicken, roaring toward each other at terrifying speed.

"I will remind you, sonny," Sarris said to Jason, "I am a general. I have seen war and death as you cannot imagine. If you are counting on me to blink, you are making a very deadly mistake."

Jason looked straight at the viewscreen. "Let me tell you something, Sarris," he said. "It doesn't take a great actor to recognize a bad one. You're *sweating*."

Indeed, a drop of sweat was dripping down Sarris's brow. Jason fixed his gaze on Sarris, and smiled.

"Armor almost gone, Jason," Gwen said worriedly.

"Ten seconds to impact," said Alexander. "Nine . . ."

"You fool," Sarris said to Jason with a smile. "What you fail to realize is that without your armor my ship will tear through yours like tissue paper."

"Well, what you fail to realize," Jason countered, "is I'm dragging mines."

Sarris's eyes filled with horror.

"*TOMMY, 270-DEGREE TURN TO PORT!*" yelled Jason.

Everybody held on as the G-forces kicked in. The *Protector* veered sharply as the mines slingshotted forward, their momentum carrying them straight toward the *Falcon*. They tore into the ship and exploded, ripping the craft apart and sending millions of fragments off into space.

On the *Protector*'s command deck, Jason stood, his clenched fist straight up in the air. The others cheered wildly.

"We did it! Damn! We did it!" they all shouted. And all over the ship, the corridors rang with the cheering of the Thermians.

The door to the command deck opened, and in came Mathesar, helped along by two of his crewmen. He was bandaged and had metal casts on an arm and leg, but he was going to be okay.

"Mathesar! You're alive—thank God!" said Jason, helping him to the commander's chair.

Mathesar looked at Jason, the old twinkle back in his eyes. Then a smile broke out on his face, and he began to laugh.

Jason stared at him with a bewildered smile. "Wha-what are you laughing about?" he said.

"'The ship is a model'!" Mathesar laughed. "'As big as this'! A very clever deception indeed!" A believer to the end, Mathesar was never going to be convinced of the truth.

Tommy smiled. "Set a course for home, Commander?" he asked.

"You can do that?" said Jason.

"It's point and click," grinned Tommy. "This thing practically flies itself. We will have to go through that black hole, though." He pointed at the swirling black hole on the viewscreen.

"Anybody have any objections?" Jason asked.

The crew exchanged shrugs. After what they had been

through already, anything else would be a piece of cake.

Only Mathesar spoke. "Won't you come with us?" he asked Jason. "There are so many challenges ahead."

"You'll be fine now," Jason told him.

"You believe this to be fact?" Mathesar asked.

"I know it," Jason assured him.

"But," Mathesar went on, "my people have no commander."

"They have a commander, Mathesar," Jason assured him, clapping his counterpart on the shoulder.

A new, confident look crossed Mathesar's face.

Jason turned to Tommy. "All right, Tommy, let's do it!"

"Commander," Tommy began.

"Yeah," Jason responded.

"Call me Laredo."

Jason smiled. "Mark Twenty into the black hole, Laredo."

They roared forward, shooting straight into the center of the black hole. The hull creaked and groaned under the strain, as if the ship was about to rip apart.

Then—silence.

Bodies turned inside out, molecules were scattered, people melted to the ground in puddles, then resolved themselves into their former shapes.

And then, *BOOOOM!* There was a loud explosion, as they were rocketed out the other end of the black hole. Planets roared past them like bullets.

"We're out!" yelled Gwen in relief.

"We're alive!" said Guy, feeling himself to make sure he was all there.

"We made it. Commander, we made it!" whooped Tommy joyously.

"By Grabthar's hammer," said Alexander softly, "we live to tell the tale."

Jason turned to look at the viewscreen. Earth was visible now, and they were hurtling toward it fast.

Alexander moved toward Jason. "Jason," he said, "before we entered the black hole, my instruments detected a strange energy surge from Sarris's ship, similar to—"

"No time to worry about that, Alex," Jason interrupted. "Tommy, let's get this thing slowed down. Gwen, see if you can calculate the impact point. Guy, get down to deck C and make sure the injured are secured. Also let's—"

He stopped speaking as he noticed the cabin door open. Fred was standing in the doorway.

Fred smiled and walked into the room. But something was just slightly off. His manner was strange. And he had a slight limp.

"Fred, what are you doing up here?" said Jason. "You should get back downstairs until we—"

Fred withdrew a magneto-pistol from his belt and leveled it at Jason.

Jason smiled, bewildered. "Fred?" he asked, as Fred fired, hitting him in the chest.

Jason took a step forward, then another, stumbling weakly toward the tech sergeant. Grabbing Fred's collar, he looked into Fred's hollow eyes a moment before collapsing to the ground. As he fell, his hand hit gadget on Fred's belt: an appearance generator.

Fred's form flickered momentarily. And then, there he was, standing there as his real, true self: Sarris. Scarred and bloody, he looked like the devil.

He raised his gun again and began firing.

Tommy was hit first, and his body went slumping over his console, pushing the thrust control full forward. The engines roared like wounded animals.

Mathesar rose, but Sarris backhanded him, sending him flying across the room. Then two Thermian crewmen tried to stop Sarris. One was shot, sent tumbling backward. Alexander and Guy ran to help the other crewman as he struggled with Sarris.

On the ground, Jason could do nothing but watch the carnage around him. He tried to rise, but it was impossible.

Sarris fired wildly, shooting Gwen as she tried to reach Jason. She fell, her body sliding down next to Jason's. Jason looked into her eyes as they dulled to lifelessness. He yelled, a huge, grief-stricken shriek, and lifted himself up with a herculean effort and began to drag himself toward the front of the room.

Next Alexander was hit. His life drifting away, he looked over to see Jason, who with supreme effort was pulling himself up on the console at the front of the room.

Meanwhile, they were still approaching Earth, and fast. There was a tremendous jolt as the ship broke through the atmosphere at twenty thousand miles an hour.

"Mathesar . . ." Jason said hoarsely.

Jason was swaying in the middle of the deck—bloody, weak, barely alive, but standing. "Activate . . . the Omega 13," he said.

Mathesar moved to the control panel and pressed a lever.
Instantly, the Omega 13 unfolded from the floor, right in
front of Jason. Its center was a spinning cyclotron of
energy. On the viewscreen, the ground rushed closer and
closer. They were just about to hurtle into the pavement
when Jason reached up and pulled the switch.

Everything went blindingly white, and completely
silent. Then, suddenly, a loud explosion like a sonic boom.

And there they all were, just as they had been thirteen
seconds ago. Gwen, Alexander, Guy, and Tommy were all
alive, busy at their stations as the *Protector* hurtled out
of the black hole.

"We're out!" yelled Gwen in relief.

"We're alive!" said Guy, feeling himself to make sure
he was all there.

"We made it. Commander, we made it!" whooped
Tommy joyously.

"By Grabthar's hammer," said Alexander softly, "we
live to tell the tale."

Jason looked around, disoriented. It took him a

moment to register what was happening. He looked down at his chest—no wounds.

The Omega 13 was real.

Jason started walking quickly across the room. Earth filled the viewscreen.

"Jason, we're going pretty fast!" Tommy called. But Jason ignored him.

"Jason?" said Gwen.

Jason continued across the room, arriving at the entrance hatch just as it opened. The others got only a glimpse of Fred's smiling face before Jason buried his fist in it. Jason pulled him up and threw him across the room. As Fred collided with a control panel, his appearance generator switch was triggered, revealing him as Sarris.

Alexander, Gwen, and the others stared, bewildered and amazed.

"Everybody stay put," said Jason. "Tommy, slow this thing down. Gwen—"

Suddenly, Sarris rose and pulled his gun. But he was smashed square in the face by a metal crutch—Mathesar's. The Thermian leader stood over Sarris with a supremely satisfied expression.

"That felt good," Mathesar added.

The crew nodded approvingly, then Guy stepped forward and trained his gun on the unconscious Sarris.

"Jason!" Tommy's voice rang out.

Jason turned and saw that the ship was hurtling

toward Earth's atmosphere. "With this weight we'll never pull out in time!" he cried.

"We must separate or we will die," Mathesar noted.

"Take your people to the secondary deck and release the command module," Jason barked out. Then he paused for a moment, realizing that this meant good-bye.

"It's the only choice," he said softly.

"Crew to the secondary!" Mathesar called out. Then he added, "Good-bye, my friends."

Gwen tuned in Fred on her monitor. "Fred, get to C level now, we're separating!" she yelled.

Fred ran through the hallway against a stream of Thermians making their way to the secondary deck. He spotted Laliari and stopped. Their eyes locked in a bittersweet moment.

Mathesar appeared by Laliari's side. He nodded at her, and she turned to follow Fred back to the command module.

Back on the command deck, Sarris's eyes snapped open. As Guy realized what was happening, Sarris grabbed the barrel of his gun and flung Guy against the wall.

Without hesitation, Jason jumped into the action. The two of them locked in life-and-death combat. Sarris pulled free and went for his knife. But they were both sent flying when the command separated from the ship. As the ship veered away, the command module continued its course straight toward Earth.

Brandon's mom and dad sat on the couch, reading the newspaper. The TV was on in the background, but nobody was really watching as a perky *E! Entertainment* reporter was relating the latest gossip. On the screen was an unflattering photo of Jason.

"Has *Galaxy Quest*'s Space Commander Jason Nesmith checked in or checked out?" she gushed. "Jim Dapperson reports form the Galaxy Con Science Fiction convention in Pasadena."

The scene cut to the reporter in front of the convention center. A group of *Galaxy Quest* fans waved at the camera behind him.

"Hi, Marsha," said Jim. "It is the third day of the Galaxy Con, and Jason Nesmith and his *Galaxy Quest* crew are all no-shows to the event, much to the disappointment the Questoids gathered here." He raised his microphone to a disappointed fan dressed in a tough warrior alien outfit.

"We just really feel let down," said the warrior alien. "I mean, part of the show is about sticking with your friends no matter what. We just feel abandoned," he added in a choked voice.

"Do you think maybe—he's in space?" Jim asked him.

"Are you mocking me?" demanded the warrior alien.

"Heh heh," said Jim, snatching back the microphone. "Digitize me, Marsha!"

Brandon's parents turned the pages of their paper, not

even watching the TV. They looked up when Brandon sped through, two boxes of July Fourth fireworks in his arms.

"Bye! Back soon!" he called, already halfway to the door.

"Wait, where are you going with those fireworks, Brandon?" his mother asked.

Brandon talked fast, rushing the whole thing out in one breath. "The *Protector* got super-accelerated coming out of the black hole and it just hit the atmosphere at Mark Fifteen, which is pretty unstable of course, so we're going to help Laredo guide it in on the vox ultrafrequency carrier and use Roman candles for visual confirmation."

"Oh. Okay, hon. Dinner at seven." She went back to the editorial page.

On the television screen, a news reporter appeared. "We interrupt this broadcast," he said, "to report that an unidentified object has broken through the Earth's atmosphere. I repeat . . ."

Mr. and Mrs. Wheeger flipped through the paper, not aware of the TV at all.

Out in the Hollywood hills, the tourists were either dumbfounded or oblivious as the mini-*Protector* came burning through the atmosphere.

In downtown L.A., hundreds of people watched, frozen, as the command module hurtled across the sky, delicately taking off the flashing tip of a light tower.

On the freeway, there was a traffic jam, as usual. Everyone was listening to the radio, as usual, when suddenly the reception went to static. And then, loud and clear, came the broadcasted transmission from the *Protector*.

"Hold course, Laredo!" cried Jason.

"I'm trying, Commander," said Tommy's voice. "Everything's a blur, but as long as I stay locked to that vox signal . . ."

"Tommy, look!" said Gwen. "Those lights!"

"I see them! I see them!"

Brandon and his team, along with a number of other heroic nerds, stood in lines on either side of Third Street in Pasadena, blobs of fire shooting from their Roman candles. Brandon stood at the front, holding his vox transmitter high.

The *Protector* capsule appeared over the horizon, gigantic and breathtaking. It came hurtling down toward the kids, hit the ground, and then slid, sparks flying. It was heading straight toward a large and familiar building: the convention center, site of the Galaxy Con.

It rocketed toward the banner which read WELCOME SPACE TRAVELERS!, then crashed right into the side of the building.

Inside the convention hall, terrified fans ran for their

lives as brick and plaster flew everywhere. The ship teetered in a cloud of dust and finally came to rest, halfway in and halfway out of the building. It had demolished the stage area.

The announcer slowly came out from under his card table. And then, the ship's main hydraulic hatch opened. A ramp lowered to the ground, and a figure emerged.

It was Tommy, looking bruised and scarred and certainly the worse for wear.

The fans didn't know how to react. In the silence, Tommy looked around the hall. Hundreds of faces looked back at him. Then they began to applaud. Tommy looked around, flabbergasted.

Then—what the heck—he waved.

The announcer hesitantly raised his microphone. "Lieutenant Laredo, Tommy Webber!" he proclaimed.

Then Gwen appeared. "The beautiful Tawny Madison, Gwen Demarco!" The fans applauded, cheered, and shouted.

Then Guy stumbled out, a cut on his head, looking disoriented. He looked out at the cheering fans.

The announcer wasn't sure who he was. "Uh . . . another shipmate!" he announced.

Guy stared out at the hundreds of faces, then a smile crept slowly onto his face.

"I'm alive," he laughed. "I'm—I'm the plucky comic relief! I'm the plucky comic relief!" His maniacal laughter was drowned out by the applause.

Then everyone's attention turned to Fred as he came down the ramp, holding hands affectionately with Laliari. "Ship's Tech Sergeant Chen, Fred Kwan, and . . . a friend!" the announcer's voice rang out.

Alexander appeared next.

"Dr. Lazarus of Tev'meck, Alexander Dane!" said the announcer.

The announcer moved to center stage and began to speak. But before he could get his words out, there was a crash. The audience looked up to see Sarris standing in the hatch. He stared out menacingly, his gun aimed at the crowd.

Then, without warning, his body fell forward in a heap. Behind him stood Jason, breathless and bloody, with Sarris's knife in his hand. In triumph, he threw down the weapon and joined his crewmates across the stage.

"Commander Peter Quincy Taggart . . . Jason Nesmith!" said the announcer. He seemed to have given up trying to figure out what to say about Sarris.

Jason, Gwen, Alexander, Fred, Tommy, and Guy stood there, shoulder to shoulder, as the audience went into a frenzy of applause. Jason looked out and spotted Brandon and his friends in the back of the room. With a look of true gratitude, Jason crossed his fists in the traditional *Galaxy Quest* gesture of respect. Brandon proudly returned it.

Then Jason dipped Gwen, giving her a big kiss. The

crowd cheered, and a teen female fan fainted. When they were done, Jason put his hands in the air, taking in the adulation.

Gwen turned to Alexander, flustered, as the audience cheered. "He always has to make the big entrance," she joked.

"By Grabthar's hammer, this is true," said Alexander. And for once, he sounded almost serious.

Epilogue

In a living room somewhere, night, a little boy, no older
than six, lay on a carpet in front of his television, kicking
his legs and munching on a bowl of popcorn. He was
watching *Galaxy Quest*. But the show looked very different now. The special effects were modern, the computer
graphics impressive. The cast credits showed the familiar
crew members, older now. And then a new one. "And
introducing Laliari as *Delilia Moon*," the credit read.

Finally, the title appeared on screen. *Galaxy Quest:
The Journey Continues*.

And as the ship whizzed out to space, the boy raised
his little fist in the air and shouted, a joyous sparkle in
his eyes:

"Never give up. Never surrender!"